"You're wearing a new perfume."

Frowning, she slanted her head to the right. His words left her confused, bewildered. *Why is Harper doing this to me?* she wondered, fiddling with her pearl necklace. *Why is he prolonging my misery?*

"What's it called?"

"Lovestruck."

"How fitting," he whispered, lowering his mouth, "because that's how I feel every time you walk into a room."

Azure felt his hands skim her breasts, and shivered when he flicked his thumb over a nipple. It was a high-voltage charge that fused her eyes to his lips, and her hands to his chest. "Stop," she croaked, hating that her order sounded more like a desperate plea. "I don't want this, and I don't want you, so—"

Harper crushed his lips to her mouth.

The kiss unleashed his desire, unleashed the pent-up emotions he'd been battling for the past two weeks. To his surprise, Azure kissed him back. Matching his heat, his urgency, she gave herself willingly to him. He sucked on her bottom lip, teased and licked it with his tongue. Her mouth felt amazing, tasted sweet, too, but didn't quench his body's thirst.

He needed more.

A *lot* more.

Books by Pamela Yaye

Harlequin Kimani Romance

PAMELA YAYE

has a bachelor's degree in Christian education, and her love for African-American fiction prompted her to pursue a career in writing romance. When she's not working on her latest novel, this busy wife, mother and teacher is watching basketball, cooking, or planning her next vacation. Pamela lives in Alberta, Canada, with her gorgeous husband and adorable but mischievous son and daughter.

Evidence
of
Desire

Pamela Yaye

HARLEQUIN®
entertain, enrich, inspire™

Pamela Yaye is acknowledged as the author of this work.

Recycling programs
for this product may
not exist in your area.

ISBN-13: 978-0-373-86277-1

EVIDENCE OF DESIRE

Dear Reader,

I hope you are enjoying this scandalous family miniseries, Laws of Love, and are anxious to read about more secrets, lies and betrayals!

In *Evidence of Desire,* attractive power couple Azure Ellison and Harper Hamilton bring the heat, as well as more drama than a reality TV show! I feel for Azure. And you will, too. Her boss is pressuring her to dig up dirt on the wealthy Hamilton clan, her image-obsessed mother is always criticizing her, and to boost her popularity she marries Harper Hamilton—a suave, sinfully sexy heartthrob she can't stop fantasizing about. What's a girl to do? Indulge in a night or two of toe-curling pleasure, that's what!

I know how much Kimani readers love scorching-hot love scenes, so I made sure Azure and Harper weren't shy about unleashing their desires in the bedroom. (Or in the kitchen. Or wherever else the mood struck!)

I love how Azure comes into her own as a woman during the course of the story, and I admire Harper's strength, his vulnerability and how he'll stop at nothing to win Azure's heart. The brother is swoonworthy for more reasons than I can count, but don't take my word for it. Read the story for yourself and see what an incredible man Harper Hamilton is.

I look forward to hearing what you think of Harper and Azure's story, so drop me a line at pamelayaye.com, or visit my Facebook page and we can discuss all your favorite juicy parts.

With love,

Pamela Yaye

I want to thank my wonderful family
for their love and support.

Special thanks to Maria Ribas
for all her hard work on *Evidence of Desire.*
It was good when I handed it in, but your suggestions
and ideas helped to make the story great! :)

Readers, this one is for you.
Thank you for your encouragement,
all those thoughtful emails you have sent me
over the years and for believing in me.
It means more than you will ever know.

Chapter 1

Harper Hamilton whacked the yellow racquetball so hard he heard his wrist crack, but when it bounced off the wall and smacked his youngest brother upside the head, he felt an odd twinge of satisfaction. *Great move, wrong family member,* he thought, wishing his cousin Jake had been on the receiving end of the powerful, unexpected blow.

"Are we cool?" Nelson asked, touching a hand to his cheek.

"Yeah, why?"

"Because that's the second time you've whacked me in the head!"

Harper wore an apologetic smile. "Sorry, man."

"You better be." Nelson coughed, flexed his jaw to make sure it wasn't broken. "This face will be worth millions one day, so take it easy, bro. I'm a budding movie star, remember?"

The brothers shared a hearty chuckle.

"I came down here to let off some steam," Harper confessed, raking a hand over his head, "but I probably should have just stayed at the office. I have depositions to read, motions to file and an important client meeting first thing tomorrow morning."

"You still pissed because Cameron Childs picked Jake to represent him instead of you?"

"No, I'm over it." Harper gripped his racket, imagined he was squeezing his cousin's neck. Thinking about how he'd been overlooked—again—for another high-profile case made his blood boil. He put in longer hours than anyone else at Hamilton, Hamilton and Clark, actively sought out new clients and had an impeccable reputation. *No John Edwards-type scandals or skeletons falling out of my closet,* he thought, dribbling the ball with his racket. *I haven't lost a case in years, so why do I keep getting passed over for the most lucrative cases?*

"I still can't believe Jake proposed to Charlotte and is about to become stepdad to a two-year-old boy," Nelson said, taking a swig from his water bottle. "If someone had told me a month ago that Jake would be engaged, I would have called them insane!"

"You and me both. I knew Jake was feeling Charlotte, but I never saw this one coming."

"No one did." Nelson added, "Well, no one besides Aunt Jeanette. Nothing gets past her!"

"I hope all the chatter dies down soon so everyone can get back to work," Harper said, cleaning the sweat off his face with the bottom of his Adidas T-shirt. Ever since Jake had gotten engaged to his paralegal, Charlotte Evans, things had been crazy around the office. Harper couldn't go anywhere without someone gushing over the couple. And he was sick of it. Sick of his colleagues congratulating Jake, patting him on the back, taking him out for celebratory after-work drinks.

"We have a huge fraud trial coming up, and there's still a lot of work that needs to be done."

"I hate to be the bearer of bad news, Harp, but no one's thinking about that fraud case anymore. The whole city is talking about Jake and Charlotte, and the only thing people care about is who's hosting their first official engagement party!"

"You'd think Jake invented the institution of marriage," Harper grumbled, folding his arms. "Charlotte's a good woman, and it's obvious Jake loves her and her son, Harry, but I don't understand why everyone's fussing over them. Couples get engaged every day. Big deal!"

Nelson chuckled. "People love a good old-fashioned love story, and I wouldn't be surprised if they made the rounds on the local TV shows, because viewers can't get enough of office romance stories."

Harper glanced at his titanium-steel sports watch and scowled when he saw the time. Premier Fitness was not only the most expensive gym in Philadelphia, but it was the busiest, and since he only had the racquetball court booked for an hour he didn't want to waste another second discussing his cousin's surprise engagement.

"Enough talk," Harper said, poised to serve. "Let's get back to our game—"

"Harper Hamilton?"

At the sound of his name, spoken on such a rich, melodious tone—one that evoked thoughts of passionate kisses, tender caresses and soulful lovemaking—he wheeled around. And when Harper saw the tall, willowy woman standing before him in the white tank top and workout shorts, the temperature in the indoor court soared to a thousand unbearable degrees.

"I'm Azure Ellison," she said, offering her right hand. "We met last month when I interviewed your family for *Eminence* magazine at—"

"My uncle's Integrity Estate," Harper finished, taking her soft, supple hand in his and giving it a light squeeze. What he really wanted to do was take her in his arms and discover once and for all if her lips tasted as sweet as they looked, but fear of getting slapped upside his head and humiliated in front of his younger brother prevented Harper from acting on his desires.

"You don't need to remind me who you are, Ms. Ellison. I know." *How could I forget? You've had a recurring role in my dreams for the past three weeks!*

"I'm flattered that you remember me."

"I never forget a face, and certainly never one as gorgeous as yours."

If only that were true, Azure thought, masking her disappointment with a fake smile. She'd been convinced that once they were alone, away from Harper's family and all of the employees crawling around the Integrity mansion, he would remember her. But Harper didn't, and for some inexplicable reason, it stung.

Azure told herself to get a grip. There was nothing to be upset about. Back in prep school, she'd been a plump, painfully shy scholarship student who didn't have a single friend, and it was silly to think that Harper Hamilton—a powerful, accomplished attorney who'd probably bedded women in the hundreds— would remember her after all these years.

"What's up? I'm Nelson. Harper's younger, devastatingly handsome brother."

Tearing her gaze away from Harper, she smiled at the aspiring actor with the piercing eyes and movie-star good looks. "It's great to finally meet you," she said, shaking the hand he offered. "I'm sorry you couldn't join us for the shoot, but I understand you were out of town."

He nodded his smooth, bald head. "I really wanted to

be there, but I had an audition for a commercial with Eva Mendes, and I couldn't pass up an opportunity to meet my favorite actress."

"And a woman you've had a giant crush on for years," Harper added, clapping his brother on the shoulder. "He watched *Hitch* so many times the DVD broke!"

The brothers laughed.

"Harper told me you're an up-and-coming writer for *Eminence* magazine, but he never mentioned how beautiful you are."

Nelson flashed his trademark grin, the one Harper had seen him use to get out of parking tickets and score tables at the best restaurants in town. "I didn't tell you she was stunning because I didn't want you to embarrass me. You know how you get when you see a drop-dead gorgeous woman!"

Azure's heartbeat wailed in her ears like a siren. *Me? Drop-dead gorgeous?* Harper couldn't be serious. He had to be playing, kidding around. Thanks to her aesthetician, she now had great skin and lush, shiny hair, but no one had ever showered her with compliments before. And more shocking still, Harper and Nelson were wearing matching smiles and staring at her intently. What was it with these Hamilton men? she wondered, fighting the urge to squeal like a schoolgirl. Why did they all have to be suave, good-looking *and* charming?

"I bet you used to model," Nelson said smoothly. "Am I right?"

No, but not for lack of trying. Azure shivered as bitter memories from her childhood resurfaced. If her mother, a former beauty queen, had had her way, she would have been a toddler in a tiara. But beauty pageants were for thin, pretty girls, and Azure had been neither. At least that was what pageant organizers repeatedly told her. Now, her younger sister, Eden, was another story. She was born to rip the runway, and from the time she could walk, she was doing just that. "No runways in my past," she replied with a nervous laugh. "I love fashion, but I was born to be a writer. It's all I've ever dreamed of doing."

Harper wore a pensive expression on his face. "That's too bad. With your look, and that million-dollar smile, you could have had a long and successful career."

"I agree," Nelson tossed in, whipping out his BlackBerry as it rang. He put it to his ear. "I better take this. It's my agent."

A grin overwhelmed Harper's mouth as he watched his kid brother exit the court. Now he finally had Azure all to himself. While they stood there, openly staring at each other, Harper allowed his eyes to do what his hands were itching to: roam over her delectable, five-foot-nine-inch frame. Her sleek black midlength bob complemented her oval face, and the side bangs that grazed her left cheek gave her a mysterious allure. Azure Ellison had lips made for kissing, hips made for squeezing and a seriously sexy vibe going on.

Casting his gaze downward, he continued his slow, thorough appraisal. Her loose-fitting workout gear hid her fit and fabulous figure, but Harper still remembered how nicely she'd filled out that black-belted-suit she'd worn to last month's photo shoot. All afternoon he'd hoped she'd ditch the stuffy blazer, but no such luck. Azure Ellison could just as easily be a model for *Eminence* magazine, and if he ever saw her striking face on the cover, he'd buy stocks in the tabloid.

Harper spotted three gangly teens leaning against the front window. They stood there, their eyes as big as saucers, jabbing each other with their elbows. Was that how he looked right now? Dazed, awed and googly-eyed? Harper hoped not. When it came to the ladies, he wasn't as confident as his cousin Jake. His ego had taken a hit when he'd caught his ex-girlfriend cheating, and Harper was only now starting to feel like his old self. Watching the trio shamelessly ogle Azure made him feel a mixture of pride and jealousy. An odd reaction considering she wasn't his woman, or even a close friend.

"I was hoping we could talk."

"Sure," he said, giving her his undivided attention, "I could spare a few minutes now."

"Not here. I'd prefer we speak in private."

"Are you in need of legal counsel, Ms. Ellison? Because if you are I'm your man."

I wish you were. Azure knew Harper was teasing, but a part of her—a big part—wished he wasn't. Lean and well built, the thirty-one-year-old attorney was an imposing figure with long, muscular limbs and a firm, hard butt she'd spent the past ten minutes drooling over. "I'm not in trouble with the law, but if I ever need an attorney, I'll be sure to give you a call."

He blessed her with a wide, disarming smile.

"Are you free tonight?"

"It depends on what this is pertaining to."

"I'm doing a follow-up piece on the interview I did last month." The lie slid smoothly off her lips. It should. She'd rehearsed it on the drive over to Premier Fitness, and again while she was working up a sweat on the elliptical machine. "I would love to sit down with you and discuss it further. Why don't we meet later for cocktails? I can tell you all about it then."

Harper raised an eyebrow. Three weeks ago, Azure had sat down with his family for an in-depth interview, one that had lasted for several hours. No way she was writing a second piece about the Hamilton clan. Only Brad and Angelina got *that* kind of coverage. "I'm afraid you're going to have to give me a little more information about this new story, Ms. Ellison."

Azure parted her lips, but nothing came out. Not a single word. Then she remembered the conversation in the staff room that morning and invented another, more compelling tale. "The whole city's buzzing with the news of your cousin's surprise engagement, and I thought it would be great to add some quotes and anecdotes about the darling couple to the piece I originally wrote. You're the first person who came to mind, so here I am."

His face hardened like stone. "I'm sorry, Ms. Ellison, but I have nothing to offer. I was just as shocked as everyone else when Jake proposed. But, if you'd like, I can arrange for you to meet with my aunt Jeannette, because she *had* to know something…."

Azure watched Harper closely, and all but fainted when he licked his full, thick lips. She admired the famed attorney from the top of his brown close-cropped hair to the bottom of his sneaker-clad feet. His skin looked as smooth as whipped peanut butter, he had a strong chiseled jaw and a pair of powerful, muscular legs. Azure longed to run her hands down his arms, wished she could touch and massage his athletic physique. Damn, and he smelled good, too. Like a rough and tough alpha male. One who could show her a thing or two in the bedroom. Or the kitchen. Or any other room he wanted to have her in.

At the thought, goose bumps prickled her flesh. Azure blinked, forced her gaze away from Harper's sexy mouth. No more lusting. It was time to refocus, to get back to the matter at hand. She had to convince Harper to meet her for drinks at Table 13, that chic, upscale restaurant bar in the heart of Center City, but how?

"I'm sorry you wasted your time coming all the way down here, but—"

"Maybe instead of writing a piece about your cousin and his new fiancée, I should feature you, *alone*," she began, casually resting a hand on his forearm. Touching him was a mistake. Her heart did a triple back flip, and Azure suddenly felt so woozy she feared she'd collapse at his feet.

What's wrong with me? Azure wondered, taking a deep breath. She'd interviewed scores of attractive men over the years, and not once did she have butterflies in her stomach or sweaty palms. But in Harper's presence she became a bumbling, stumbling fool who couldn't think straight. *What's up with that?*

Seconds passed before she felt composed enough to speak. Once her head cleared, she continued her pitch. "I'd love to discuss my idea further with you, and if you could spare an hour of your time to meet with me tonight I'd really appreciate it."

"Just tell me when and where." His smile was back, and his dark, penetrating gaze moved over her like the fierce autumn breeze blowing leaves outside the downtown streets. Azure didn't have the presence of mind to think, let alone speak. Harper Hamilton had it all. Dashing good looks, keen intelligence and a physique that would make an action hero jealous. And he did it for her in a big way. "Let's meet at Table 13," she said, breaking free of her sinful thoughts and reuniting with her voice. "Is seven o'clock okay?"

"It's perfect."

"Great. I'll see you then."

"I look forward to it."

Azure's legs were shaking, but she turned around and walked across the racquetball court without wiping out. *How the hell am I going to make it through cocktail hour with Harper when I could barely handle a five-minute conversation?* she thought, hustling back through the lobby of Premier Fitness and out the front door. Azure had a date to get ready for, and no time to waste. She only hoped that between now and the time she met Harper for cocktails at Table 13, she had a new plan because her first one had just been shot to hell.

Chapter 2

At six o'clock, Azure sailed into Table 13 and after a brief chat with the curvy, blue-eyed hostess, strode through the packed-out waiting area. The word *swank* came to mind every time Azure entered Philly's newest hot spot, but after attending last month's grand opening, she quickly realized that all that glittered wasn't gold. Table 13 was a place to see and be seen in. That was it. The ceilings were high, and the décor flashy, but the overpriced entrées were smaller than a Mc-Donald's Happy Meal and the service was painfully slow. But the scathing reviews by local critics didn't deter the crowds. In the lounge, dozens of young, fabulously dressed patrons with money to burn and not a care in the world sipped champagne and smoked cigars.

Azure was an hour early for her meeting with Harper, but she planned to use the time to develop her new plan. She hoped that once she had a couple of cocktails, and her nerves settled, the ideas would flow freely, because right now she had nothing. Mr. Watson's words circled her mind, and although it had been hours since her boss had marched into her office and reamed her out, she could still hear his harsh voice in her ears. *"Shape up or ship out, Ellison. And for goodness' sake, quit writing boring fluff pieces that your own mother wouldn't read!"*

Sliding onto the swivel stool in her slim-fitting Gucci dress took more skill than winning *Jeopardy's* Tournament of Champions, but once Azure was seated at the bright, circular bar, she felt herself start to relax. The bartender smiled at her, and as he approached, Azure decided she had nothing to worry about. She looked good, felt even better and had a feeling Harper would open up to her. *Or at least that's my hope,* she thought, reaching for one of the drink lists displayed beside the decorative napkin holder.

"Funny seeing you here...."

Azure glanced to her right. When she saw Harper, sitting two seats over, her eyes widened. Her heart fluttered like a butterfly, and when his gaze moved over her with deliberate slowness, her lips parted wordlessly. Realizing how utterly ridiculous she must look, Azure closed her mouth and wiped the dreamy, love-struck expression off her face. "You're early."

"So are you."

Harper gestured to his iPad. "I thought I'd get some work done while I watched the Sixers game. What's your excuse?"

"I was planning to work, too," she lied, nervously combing a lock of hair behind her ears. "I have a deadline fast approaching, and as usual I'm hopelessly behind."

"Let me buy you a drink."

The deep timbre of his voice, and the way he was staring at her, made it impossible for Azure to speak. Not in complete sentences, anyway.

"What would you like?"

To kiss you. Desire singed her flesh. Azure shook the outrageous thought from her mind. Clearly, being in close proximity to this gorgeous corporate attorney was wreaking havoc on her good sense. But smart, intelligent guys with perfect teeth and great bodies had always been her weakness, and Harper Hamilton was the prototype of her dream guy. Only he wasn't a dream. He was a living, breathing hunk of a man who smelled divine. "I'll have a Coke," she told the pierced bartender, when he sidled up to her. "No, on second thought, make that a dry martini."

"Good choice." Harper raised his glass. "That's what I'm having."

Azure nodded, watched as he packed up his leather briefcase and set it on the floor. His rich, wonderful fragrance wrapped itself around her in a sweet, sensual hug, and, oh, did he ever look good, too! Azure loved his casual, polished style and had a hell of a time keeping her eyes off his body and on her menu. Harper was off the clock, but he still looked like an acclaimed attorney at the top of his game. His white dress shirt and eye-catching burgundy tie warmed his flawless, smooth complexion, his dark slacks were tailored to perfection and his diamond wristwatch outshone the chandelier hanging above the bar.

Anxious to get down to business, she gestured to the dining area with her hand. "We should probably go grab a table. It's starting to fill up in here."

"I'm fine here at the bar, if you are. There's a line down the block to get in, and I'm not interested in waiting outside." Harper glanced at the floor-to-ceiling windows. "I used to deliver flyers when I was a teenager, and to this day, every time I have to walk more than a block or two I moan and grumble!"

"You had a part-time job in high school?"

"You mean *jobs,*" he corrected, chuckling good-naturedly. "My parents wanted me to understand the value of a dollar, so once I was old enough they encouraged me to work. Or rather, forced me to! I shoveled snow, mowed lawns, walked dogs. I did it all, and hated every minute of it."

"Now I don't feel so bad about working at Fat Burger. At least I wasn't outside!"

"You used to work at Fat Burger? Wow, back in the day that place was my second home." He wore a wistful expression, but his tone was filled with humor. "There was one across the street from my prep school, and my friends and I would head over there whenever we had a spare. I had the same thing every day. A—"

"Triple King Meal, ten-piece chicken nuggets and a chocolate milkshake."

"Yeah," he said, raising a thick, perfectly groomed eyebrow. "How did you know?"

Azure shifted around on her stool. "Just a lucky guess. I worked at Fat Burger for years, and that seemed to be everybody's favorite."

"You're probably right. My buddies ordered the same thing, too."

In the lounge, chuckles rang out, the scent of fresh garlic bread filled the air and patrons danced to the pop song playing. When the bartender returned to refresh their drinks, Harper ordered an appetizer platter and a bottle of wine.

"I hope you're eating for two," Azure quipped, hiding a smirk that threatened to overwhelm her mouth, "because that platter serves six and I'm not hungry."

"Don't tell me you're one of those weight-obsessed, calorie-counting types who's strict about what she eats."

"Isn't every woman?"

Harper tasted his drink, then rested it on his coaster. "It's not the size of a woman's waist or the length of her hair that makes her beautiful. It's how she carries herself, how confident and comfortable she is in her skin. I've dated sisters of all shapes and sizes and—"

"You have?"

"Of course, I'd be a fool not to. Contrary to what the fashion industry thinks, beauty comes in plus-size packages, too, and I'm tired of only seeing toothpick-thin models on billboards and magazine covers." He wore a smile. "No offense."

Azure held up her hands. "None taken. And I agree with you. I've been pushing the powers-that-be at *Eminence* to hire more full-figured models, but my new boss, Leland Watson, isn't on board. All he cares about is turning the magazine into a glossier, more scandalous version of *People* magazine."

"On that note, I'd love to hear more about the piece you're working on."

You and me both, Azure thought, clearing her throat. Facing him, she arched her shoulders and crossed her legs. Sucking in her stomach hurt, but she clasped her hands around her knees and wore a winning smile. Perfect. Now he couldn't see her hands shaking.

"I must admit, I was shocked when you asked me to meet you here tonight."

"You were? Why?"

"Because you're a beautiful woman who I'm sure has no shortage of admirers."

Azure felt her eyes bulge out of her head. *Harper thinks I'm beautiful? For real? No way!* The idea was shocking, mind-boggling, as unbelievable as shoulder pads coming back in style, but Harper looked dead serious. His gaze was intense, smoldering with such heat, her heart skipped two beats. For a split second, Azure considered telling Harper who she was. It was obvious he didn't remember her, so why not come clean?

Because if I confess to being frumpy ol' Alice Ellison, it might ruin my chances with him.

Shaking her head helped Azure come to her senses. She

had to be professional. This was business. Strictly business. And once she gained Harper's trust and tricked him into revealing family secrets, she'd be on her way because being around this strong, virile attorney was too much temptation for a single, celibate girl like herself to take. "My boss wants me to produce a story that breaks new ground, a piece that will get the whole country talking, and I think I may have found what he's looking for. But to write the story, I need to interview someone inside the Hamilton family dynasty."

"And that would be me," he offered, his expression guarded, his tone tight.

Azure nodded. To lighten the mood and put him at ease, she spoke from the heart. "We're a lot alike, you and me, and I think—"

"Is that so? In what way, Ms. Ellison?"

"For starters, we're both keen observers who don't automatically buy what we've been told. We're hard workers who never take the easy way out, but we're often overshadowed by louder, flashier colleagues who believe their own hype."

Harper stroked his jaw reflectively. He was impressed. Azure Ellison had described him to a T. No one had ever done that before, but the longer he stared at her, the more convinced he was that she was hiding something. There was something familiar about her, mysterious, too. Was it possible they'd met before last month's photo shoot? Through an acquaintance or business associate maybe? Instead of playing a solitary game of twenty questions, he decided to lay his cards on the table. "Who are you *really,* Azure Ellison, and what are you after?"

"I sensed a bit of animosity between you and Jake during last month's interview," Azure said, sidestepping his question. "I'm curious if there was more to that argument I witnessed than you led me to believe."

His eyes narrowed, lost their luster and the veins in his neck pulsed.

Bingo! Tempering her excitement, she paused to taste her cocktail and waited a half second before moving in for the kill. "I'd love to profile you, Harper. *Just you.* We could do a full-page spread with pictures, quotes and a list of your most high-profile cases."

Interest sparked in Harper's eyes as he straightened in his seat.

"I suspect that you're the unsung hero of the firm, and I'd love to give you a chance to tell the world what's really going on behind the scenes at Hamilton, Hamilton and Clark."

Azure was spinning her tale as fast as she could, saying and doing all the right things, but Harper didn't respond. He looked amused, as if he were watching a kitten chase its tail around in circles, and his broad grin was growing by the second. "Will you do the interview?"

Several long, tense seconds ticked by.

"I'll do it, but only if you agree to have dinner with me tomorrow."

"Lunch," she countered. "In my office on Friday."

"Dinner. Six o'clock sharp."

"Brunch. Eleven-thirty."

Harper wore an arch grin. "Tomorrow night. The Clearwater Grill on Sixth Street."

"Why not somewhere around here or in Mount Airy?"

"Because I'd love a good steak, and no one does it better than the head chef at the Clearwater Grill on Sixth."

Azure frowned. "Really? I've heard of the place, but I've never been there."

"You'll love it. Everyone does. It's quiet, the service is great and the manager is the funniest guy you'll ever meet."

"I'd rather interview you in my office. It's a more professional setting and we won't have to worry about being interrupted or distracted."

"The Clearwater Grill," he repeated, his tone calm, cool. "Take it or leave it."

"I'll be there."

What just happened? Azure thought sourly, wishing she hadn't given in so easily. *That went* real *well, Azure. Are you sure you're the one in charge?* She was beating herself up for giving Harper the upper hand when she caught sight of a slight man in a striped fedora and matching sports coat in the waiting area.

Azure blinked hard, tried to get a better look at the stranger's profile. Perspiration drenched her palms and clung to her dress. No. It couldn't be. Her boss wouldn't do something as sneaky as spying on her, would he? A former tabloid reporter, with a remarkable gift for sniffing out the truth, Leland Watson was as cunning as he was brilliant, and he never let her forget it. He was an acclaimed journalist, and well respected in the field, but Azure wouldn't put anything past him. And the more she considered it, the more likely it *was* her boss in the tacky fedora and sports coat. After all, he'd asked—no, ordered—her to track down Harper and been the one to suggest they meet for cocktails at Table 13, too.

Azure peered over Harper's shoulder. The stranger strode through the bar, and when he disappeared into the lounge and out of sight, she released a sigh of relief. Hopefully someone rich and famous had caught his eye. Either way, it was time to call it a night. She had a long day ahead of her, and now a brand-new interview with Harper to prepare for. It wasn't time to sit pretty. It was time to go on the attack. And when she met with the famed attorney tomorrow night, that was exactly what she was going to do.

"See someone you know?" Harper asked, sliding several

crisp bills into the leather billet. "Or are you trying to get a better look at Drake and his ten-man entourage?"

Azure dismissed his question with a wave of her hand. "Drake's cute, but he's way too young for me. Besides, I like my men the way I like my coffee. Strong and dark."

Harper rocked with laughter. "I'll keep that in mind."

"You do that, Mr. Hamilton."

"Call me Harper."

"Only if you call me Azure."

He nodded, leaned in so close she could smell his spicy, masculine cologne. "So, what do you do when you're not working?"

"I'm always working. Aren't you?"

Another hearty chuckle. "Yes, but I make time to hang out with my family, to watch my beloved Seventy-Sixers and I travel several times a year. You should see my passport. It looks like a dog's chew toy!"

"I'm so jealous. I've never left the States, and all the travel I do is for work."

"I'll have to do something about that, then."

Their eyes caught, and held, and Azure was so overcome by the intensity of Harper's gaze and his heady scent that all she could do was stare at him.

"You should come with me to the Cabo San Lucas Music Festival. I go every year, and the concerts, cuisine and atmosphere are out of this world." Harper added, "But don't take my word for it, come and see for yourself."

"My boss will never give me the time off." Azure felt guilty for lying to Harper—again—but she didn't feel comfortable sharing her business with him. She couldn't afford to go to Cabo, or anywhere else for that matter. Not until she paid off her bills. But Harper had given her something to think about. A trip to the famed celebrity hot spot sounded divine, something worth planning once she straightened out her finances.

"Is there a special man in your life anxiously waiting for you to return home?"

Azure was caught off guard by the question, but she didn't show it. "No, just my cats."

"Your cats?"

"Yup, Darius and Lovehall."

Harper thought for a moment, then released a deep, hearty chuckle. "You named your cats after the male character in *Love Jones?*"

"I sure did."

"You must really like the movie."

"Who doesn't? It's one of the greatest romantic movies of all time!"

"The movie came out when I was in high school, and my female classmates went wild for Larenz Tate. The editor of the school newspaper even devoted an issue to the movie."

Azure couldn't believe it. Harper remembered the column she'd done for the school newspaper? Who would have thought? He didn't recognize her, but he remembered her article, and that made her feel proud. Although they'd never had any classes together or traveled in the same social circles, Harper had always greeted her when they'd passed each other in the halls. And once, when she'd been caught in a rainstorm, he'd been kind enough to share his umbrella with her.

Azure remembered that afternoon as if it were yesterday. Outwardly, she'd remained calm as they'd stridden toward the tree-lined campus side by side, but inside Azure had been a maelstrom of emotion. Fear, excitement and sheer, unadulterated joy. They'd walked and talked, and although her legs had been shaking under her painfully tight school uniform, she'd held up her end of the conversation. After that, Harper Hamilton—the upperclassman voted most likely to one day be president—starred in all her teenage fantasies. Once he graduated and went off to law school, Azure never saw him again, but every time it rained, she wondered what had happened to the kind, great-looking guy who'd shared his umbrella with her.

Memories flooded her mind, and when Azure thought about the day she arrived at Bryn Mawr College, a smile warmed her face. Studying at the highly acclaimed women's college was the best thing to ever happen to her. During her sophomore year, she'd shed some weight, traded her hideous, Coke-bottle-thick glasses for contacts and found her confidence, her voice. Azure made friends with her *über*-rich classmates and soon discovered that brains always trumped breeding. In the space of a year, she went from being a novice reporter to an editor of the school newspaper and ultimately editor in chief. After graduation, and a series of starts and stumbles, *Eminence* magazine hired her, and once she changed her first name to Azure her career took off like a meteorite.

Pride filled her. Life was good. Better than she could ever have imagined. She was sitting across from Harper Hamilton in the most exclusive restaurant in Philly, and he was flirting with her! Azure wanted to pinch herself. The attorney had *it*. Charisma, charm, that indescribable quality that drove women wild. He had it in spades, and there was something so powerful between them, something so crushing, her head was spinning.

"I hope what I'm about to say doesn't offend you, Azure, but you look amazing in that dress. It's sexy but tasteful and the emerald-green color is perfect for the season."

Azure raised her eyebrows in a questioning slant. "Don't tell me you're a male fashionista," she teased, unable to resist poking fun at him. "You're a great dresser, but I pegged you more as a sports guy than a shop-till-you-drop one."

"You're right, I am, but my mom is a fashion designer and I've learned a thing or two from her over the years. We all have. My brothers, my cousins, even my dad, and he used to live in cheap, tacky polyester!"

Harper stood, slid up behind her and when he rested a hand on her lower back, her knees went weak—again. *Damn it, why does that keep happening?*

"Let me walk you to your car."

"I'd like that," she said, taking the hand he offered and easing carefully off her stool. *I'm also dying to know if you're a good kisser, but for now, the walk will do.*

Chapter 3

Rittenhouse Square, a popular neighborhood named after the large, lush, tree-filled park in the center of the community, was overrun with residents taking advantage of the unusually warm October day. From his fourth-floor office window, Harper had a clear, unrestricted view of the park and marveled at how crowded it was. Joggers ran along the winding, leaf-covered path, kids darted around the jungle gym and pet owners played catch with their dogs.

On Thursday afternoons, Harper liked to go outside to the square. For an hour, he'd sit back and relax. He wouldn't think about work and the long list of things he had to accomplish before quitting time, either. He'd eat his lunch, then do the *New York Times* crossword puzzle. But not today. Harper had a deposition to review, phone calls to make and more paper crowding his desk than a UPS office.

Harper tossed a handful of cashews into his mouth. *Five more minutes, and then I'll get back to work,* he told himself, soaking up the sunshine pouring through the window in front of his L-shaped executive desk. Most of the offices at Hamilton, Hamilton and Clark were furnished traditionally, with mahogany furniture and Oriental rugs, but Harper had bucked the trend and hired an interior decorator to create his dream space. Leather couches sat along one wall, shelves displaying his certificates and awards were above the tropical-fish aquarium, and his favorite electronic gadgets were just an arm's length away on the decorative glass stand.

Crossing his legs at his ankles, he rested back comfortably in his seat. He spotted a group of teenagers reading magazines under one of the leafy maple trees dotting the park, and immediately thought of Azure. The writer had been on his mind all day. Actually, ever since the photo shoot at his uncle's estate. He was looking forward to seeing her tonight, and as soon as he finished drafting the settlement letter, he was heading home. He needed to shower and change before their date, and he wanted to buy Azure flowers from his favorite gift shop. Not that he went there often. Harper hadn't been back to Gifts & Things since...

Scraping the thought and all images of his ex-girlfriend from his mind, he turned away from the window and picked up the manila file folder he'd abandoned ten minutes earlier.

"I thought you'd left for the day."

Harper regarded his father, Frank, with a smile. His dad was fifty-eight years old and still going strong. He not only looked years younger, but he played the part, too. His dad was a jovial, well-dressed ball of energy who was always in a terrific mood. In court, he rarely sat down, and when he did it was only because his back was acting up. "I have a few more things to do before I head home," Harper explained, gesturing to the document in his hands, "and since I'm in court tomorrow, I figured now was as good a time as any to get them done."

"I was surprised when I pulled into the parking lot this morning and saw your car. What time did you get in?"

"Five-thirty. I would have been here earlier but decided to go to the gym first."

"Some people shouldn't be allowed to drink coffee," Frank joked, pointing at his son's oversize Philadelphia Sixers-themed mug. "You'd be one of them!"

Father and son chuckled.

"What are you working on?" Frank asked, closing the door behind him.

"Just reviewing the sworn testimony of the victims in the fraud case. The trial is fast approaching, and I want to be fully prepared."

"Good, good, son. That's what I like to hear." Frank picked up the golf club that Harper kept in his office for his executive putter set, pointed it at the cup and bent his knees. "I wish I had one of these in my office, but if I did I'd probably never get any work done!"

Harper watched as his father practiced his swing. Over and over, he took shots at the hole. Harper didn't know if his dad came by to see him or to play a round of golf, but he didn't mind the interruption. He welcomed it. Maybe shooting the breeze with his dad would help him refocus, because he was so amped up about seeing Azure again he couldn't concentrate.

"Son, when are you heading home?"

"I'm not sure, why?"

"Preseason basketball kicks off tonight," Frank said, glancing up from the golf set. "The Lakers are playing in Miami tonight, and there's been so much trash talking between the two teams, I wouldn't be surprised if there was a brawl in the first quarter!"

"I thought Mom banned you from watching basketball."

"The Lakers got swept in the second round of the playoffs!

Swept!" he repeated, throwing a hand up in the air. "It's not my fault I got so angry I bumped into the coffee table and knocked over that frilly candy dish. It's been six months and I *still* haven't got over it."

Harper chuckled.

"Besides, what your mother doesn't know can't hurt her," Frank said, shooting his son a wink. "She's in New York on business, so I have the house all to myself this week."

A sly grin exploded onto his dad's smooth, slim face, but Harper heard the loneliness in his voice and saw the flicker of sadness in his eyes. Harper considered canceling his date with Azure. He was anxious to pick up where they'd left off last night, but he didn't want to leave his old man hanging.

"Your brothers are coming by, and some of your cousins, too."

"Will Jake be there?"

Frank shrugged. "I invited him, but I don't know if he'll show. He has a meeting tonight with Santiago Medina."

In his haste to speak, Harper tripped over his tongue. "The resort heir?"

"The one and only. Apparently, Mr. Medina is looking for a new, American-based lawyer, and after speaking to Jake on the phone last week, he decided to fly in on his family's private jet for a face-to-face meeting."

Harper's heart sank to the bottom of his leather Kenneth Cole shoes. Jake had scored another big-name client? And not just anyone. One of the richest businessmen in all of Mexico. Harper was pissed, but he didn't show it. He couldn't let his dad, or anyone else, know that he was jealous. Harper loved Jake, and would never do him any harm, but he was tired of playing second string to his flashy, cocky cousin. "Why would Santiago Medina sign with Jake? He's arrogant, obnoxious and—"

"One hell of a closer," Frank added, picking up the golf

club and lining up his feet on the putter. "You're an incredible attorney, son, the best in the firm as far as I'm concerned, but you need to toughen up. You lack that killer instinct that all great attorneys have, and without it, you can only go so far in this business. It doesn't matter if you're closing a deal, or trying to get a babe into bed, when you see an opening, you have to go in for the kill."

Harper wanted to plug his ears. He didn't want to hear what was coming next. His dad—like most of the Hamilton men—loved women, and back in the day had had a reputation with the ladies. Always on the move, he laughed, joked and flirted with the opposite sex as if it was his favorite pastime. And Harper suspected it was.

"I know you don't want to hear this, but you could learn a thing or two from Jake."

"On what? How to seduce and bed my paralegal?"

"No, on how to get more bang for your buck! Jake's parlayed his engagement into a huge news story and is attracting wealthy clients left and right."

Harper's shoulders slumped, caved in under the weight of his disappointment. Feelings of resentment and despair filled him. He couldn't believe it. Now his father, the person who'd always been his biggest supporter, had jumped on the I-love-Jake bandwagon, too. *And the president thinks* he's *got it bad,* Harper thought sourly, stewing in his leather executive chair.

"I better get going," Frank said, glancing at the wall clock. He returned the golf club to its rightful place, then checked himself out in the mirror hanging beside the wardrobe. "My next client is due to arrive at any moment, and I don't want to keep him waiting."

Long after his father left, Harper sat at his desk, thinking. He wondered what it would take to upstage his cousin Jake, because he was sick of being the number two guy at Hamilton, Hamilton and Clark. It was time for him to shine, time for him to represent the firm's big-dollar clients. Harper was nothing if not focused, and tonight, after his date with Azure, he was going to sit down and prepare a plan of action. He had to do something to steal the spotlight away from Jake, something that would garner national headlines. The only question now was what?

"Is this seat taken?"

Harper glanced up from his cell phone. A redhead with fake eyelashes and glossy lips was standing beside his booth, smiling so brightly Harper wished he was wearing sunglasses.

"Yes, as a matter of fact it is."

"Then I'll be brief." The redhead slid in beside him, got so close he could feel her double Ds pressed against his forearm. "I saw you interviewed outside the courthouse last night on the evening news, and I just had to come over and say hello. I'm, like, your biggest fan!"

Harper wanted to send the buxom redhead on her way, but he nodded and produced a winning smile. Had to keep the public happy. Hamilton, Hamilton and Clark had been founded in 1960 by his grandfather, Jacob Hamilton Sr., and his business associate, Albert Clark, but these days the firm was more popular than ever. Harper enjoyed all the perks that came with being a Hamilton, but he could do without the aggressive gold diggers and so-called fans. This was the third woman who'd approached him since he arrived at the Clearwater Grill and she was by far the pushiest. The small, cozy restaurant was overrun with love-struck couples, but there were plenty of scantily clad women out on the prowl.

"The cameras don't do you justice, Harper. You're even sexier in person."

"Ah, thanks."

"On the news, they said your client was awarded a half-million-dollar settlement. I bet that's chump change to you, I mean, you *are* a Hamilton…."

Harper didn't want to talk about the sexual harassment case he'd won last week, or his family's staggering net worth, either. All he wanted to do was sip his cappuccino in peace while he waited for his date to arrive. The last thing Harper wanted was for Azure to walk in and spot him talking to this Pamela Anderson look-alike, so he slid to the edge of the booth.

Harper glanced over at the waiting area and strangled a groan. Too late. Azure was standing at the entrance of the lounge, and she was staring right at him. "It was nice meeting you, miss. Enjoy the rest of your evening." Grabbing his cell phone, he leaped to his feet as if the booth were on fire and took off before the redhead could give chase.

As he approached Azure, he fought the overwhelming urge to kiss her, to caress her flawless brown skin. She looked sensational from head to foot, and her lush, scarlet-red lips were tempting. So tempting, in fact, kissing her was all he could think about. For the past six months, his life had been an endless stream of business meetings, and the thought of spending the rest of the night with Azure Ellison excited him.

Instead of succumbing to his needs and planting one on her, Harper settled for a peck on the cheek. She smelled delicious, heavenly, as intoxicating as a bottle of Herbal Essences shampoo, and thinking about those infamous shower-scene commercials made Harper wonder what Azure was like in bed. He'd bet that she was vocal, confident, a woman who didn't hold back, who gave as good as she got.

A grin claimed his lips. Maybe if he played his cards right tonight he'd find out. The thought stunned him. Harper hadn't had sex in months, hadn't wanted to—until now. The pain of being betrayed by his ex—a woman he'd been prepared to spend the rest of his life with—ran deep, and until five minutes ago, he hadn't given anyone a second glance. But there was something about Azure Ellison, something about her that appealed to him on a physical and intellectual level. And it didn't hurt that her figure was a thing of beauty. Everything about the magazine reporter was sexy. Her lush hair, her lean arms and hips, the graceful way she moved through space. Harper was burning up, so blinded by his attraction to her he narrowly missed crashing into the lanky busboy cleaning tables. An ice pack in his boxer briefs wouldn't cool him down, and when Azure smiled at him, his blood pressure spiked and his skin felt hotter than the flames crackling in the stone fireplace.

Azure looked Harper over. Not once, not twice, but three shameless times. His argyle sweater fit his very sexy, very gorgeous body perfectly, and his dark slacks accentuated his long, lean legs. Looking casual but polished was an art, and Harper Hamilton was the master. His smile, his energy and those warm brown eyes got her every time. And obviously she wasn't the only one. The redhead sitting in the lounge was staring longingly at him, like a woman desperately and hopelessly in love.

"Harper, my man, great to see you!"

Nodding at Louis, the affable restaurant owner with the moustache and slicked-down black hair, he said, "Likewise, sir. How are things?"

"Great, great, can't complain. What have you been up to? It's been months since you paid us a visit," he complained, wearing a forlorn face.

"Work's been keeping me busy."

Louis grinned like a leprechaun with a pot of gold. "Work? Or this gorgeous woman standing beside you?"

"Azure is stunning, isn't she?"

"You can say that again."

Harper slid his arm around her waist, held on tight. A thousand volts of electricity rushed through Azure's body. Why did that keep happening? she wondered, trying to ignore the fluttering sensation in the pit of her stomach. Azure didn't know what was wrong with her. She was a bold, confident, take-charge kind of sister, but around Harper she became a different person. Shy, skittish, as nervous as an Amish girl on her first date. And the more Harper flirted with her, the more her hands and legs shook.

"Your girlfriend caused quite a stir when she walked in. My cooks were so busy checking her out they bumped into each other and spilled appetizers all over the floor!"

"Then you better find us a quiet, secluded table *far* away from the kitchen," Harper joked, clapping a hand on the restaurant owner's shoulders, "because they're liable to burn the whole kitchen down if we sit out here!"

Azure lost the use of her tongue and the ability to form words. She waited for Harper to correct the manager, to explain that they weren't a couple, but he didn't. Instead, he requested his favorite table and led her into the dining area. The cream-and-beige space was outfitted with candlelit round tables, a stone fireplace showered the room with warmth and the padded leather booths along the far wall were large enough to fit an entire basketball team. The restaurant had the perfect ambience for romance or a clandestine magazine interview, and once their orders were placed and their drinks arrived, Azure got right down to business.

"I appreciate you meeting me tonight," she said, setting her tape recorder on the table and her trusty notebook on her lap. "I know you're a very busy man with no time to waste, so I'll try my best to keep my questions brief and to the point."

"Why don't we talk first, off the record, and do the interview after dinner?"

"Or we can do it now while we wait for our entrées to arrive," Azure countered, hoping he didn't hear the apprehension in her voice. Her mind was fuzzy, and she had a hell of a time meeting his gaze. Azure didn't know if she was feeling light-headed because of the delicious scent of Harper's cologne or because he was studying her so intently. Either way, she had to get it together, and quick. Azure had a lot riding on this interview—her career, her reputation, a job she loved more than anything in the world—and couldn't afford to blow this opportunity.

Determined to uncover the "dirt" her boss was dying for, she took a deep, cleansing breath and pushed the record button on the tape recorder. "Let's get started, shall we?"

"Ask away, Azure. I have nothing to hide."

Guilt pricked her heart. *I wish I could say the same.*

Chapter 4

Harper felt short of breath, as if he'd just finished swimming a dozen laps, and every time he caught a whiff of Azure's sweet, floral perfume, his brain short-circuited. Pounded, spun, whirled faster than a helicopter propeller. He saw her lips moving, heard her rich, dulcet tone in his ears, but he didn't understand a word she was saying. It took supreme effort, but Harper forced his gaze away from her luscious mouth and back up to her pretty brown eyes.

"What is it like working at one of the most prestigious law firms in the country?"

Pride filled him and seeped into his voice. "I love what I do, and I feel honored to be working at my family's law firm," he said smoothly, folding a leg across his knee. "When I was a little boy, my father used to take me with him to court, and the first time I ever saw him deliver closing arguments, I was sold. I knew right then and there I was going to be an attorney."

"What do you like most about your job?"

"You mean besides winning big cases?" A grin exploded onto his lips. "I love the intellectual challenge of the law and liken the profession to chess, but with real and very flawed people. The player with the best interpretation of the law usually wins, and I'm proud to say that more often than not it's Hamilton, Hamilton and Clark."

"It's obvious you love what you do, but there must be some things you don't like…."

Harper thought for a moment, then answered truthfully, "The hours are incredibly long, and there's a lot of repetition. Being a lawyer is nowhere near as glamorous as it looks on TV, and the competition inside the law firm is fierce. Everyone wants to make a name for themselves, no matter the cost."

Listening to him, Azure got the sense that he was angry about something, and decided to play her hunch. "Are you and your cousin Jake fierce rivals?"

"I don't know. You tell me."

His response confused her, so she rephrased the question, hoping this time Harper would give her a straight answer instead of being as evasive as a secret agent. "Would you say Jake is your stiffest competition at the firm?"

"That depends. Is he vying for your affection, too?"

Azure's cheeks burned, felt hotter than the tip of a flame. Searching his face for the truth, she tried to decipher if he was teasing her or being serious. Harper looked relaxed, completely at ease, like a man who had the world at his feet. But he wasn't a cocky, swaggering rich guy who thought he was better than everyone else. Azure appreciated how humble he was, how courteous and well mannered. Harper Hamilton was it, and he didn't even know it. There was nothing sexier than an intelligent, ridiculously handsome man with great manners, and Harper possessed all of those qualities and more.

"I'm sorry if I embarrassed you, Azure. Sometimes when

I'm around a beautiful woman, I lose my head, but I'm sure you're used to men tripping all over themselves. I guess that's the price you have to pay for being stunning."

Azure was surprised as anything when Harper touched her hand. And like the morning sun on a hot, balmy summer day, his smile felt warm and hot on her face. Azure couldn't stop staring at him, couldn't peel her eyes away. Forget Kobe Bryant and Lebron James. Harper Hamilton had *serious* game, and if she wasn't careful, she'd end up shaming herself and the entire female population by acting on her desires.

"It's been a long time since I went out with anybody, and I'm really enjoying your company, Azure. It's so easy to be around you, and you have a terrific sense of humor. I like that. And I like you."

Azure pushed on, pretended his comment had no effect on her. Even though it did. Her heart raced, beat in double time. There was something in the air, something so powerful, Azure knew she'd never be the same again. She drew a breath, one that should have steadied her nerves but didn't. "Tell me more about what happens behind the scenes at Hamilton, Hamilton and Clark," Azure said, pulse pounding, limbs shaking. Taking a quick sip of her drink, she watched as Harper unzipped his sports coat, took it off and draped it behind his chair. As if she didn't have enough problems. Now she'd have to try not to stare at his broad, muscular chest. "Surely, you're not one big happy family twenty-four-seven."

"No, you're certainly right about that, we're not. Colleagues argue and bicker in every profession, and it's no different at Hamilton, Hamilton and Clark. I hate to admit it, but sometimes it's hard to believe we're family."

"It is?"

Harper gave a solemn nod. "Working with family members presents its own unique set of problems, and I'd be lying if I said things don't get heated from time to time. We fight, we argue and on occasion we even…"

Azure wet her lips. This was going better than expected! Harper was actually opening up to her, revealing family secrets. By the time they wrapped up the interview she'd have everything she needed for her story and more.

"My dad and my uncle Jacob are always cursing someone out, and just last week Jake got into a fistfight with Griffin Jackson, one of our sharpest and brightest attorneys."

Scandalous, Azure thought, cheering inwardly. This was exactly what her boss was looking for, the kind of juicy gossip that readers wanted to eat for breakfast, lunch and dinner.

"Once, I even walked in on…"

"Uh-huh." Azure inched forward, got nice and close so she wouldn't miss what Harper was about to divulge. "Once, you walked in on…"

"My cousin Marissa locked in a passionate embrace with one of our *very* married clients. I was so stunned I stumbled out of the room and back down the hall to my office."

Frowning, Azure stopped writing on her trusty notepad. That was hard to believe. No, impossible. She had a knack for reading people, and Marissa Hamilton was no Long Island Lolita. Petite and slender, she looked more like a teenager than a hard-boiled attorney, and during last month's interview she'd graciously answered each question and spoken openly about the pressure of being the youngest attorney at the family law firm. No way she'd ever fool around with a client, single or otherwise.

"And that's not all. Wait until I tell you what my dad did at last year's Christmas party!"

"You're making this stuff up as you go along, aren't you?" Azure glared at him, made a face she hoped conveyed her disgust. "I can't believe you've been feeding me lies this entire time. You agreed to this interview and promised to answer my questions truthfully."

"I'm not the only one playing games, though, am I?"

Her head pounded louder than her heartbeat.

"I've met your boss, Leland Watson, at several social events around town, and he strikes me as an ambitious but very difficult man."

You could say that again, Azure thought, remembering the tongue-lashing he'd given her in his office the day before yesterday. If she didn't love her job, and the extraordinary group of people she worked with, she would have quit a long time ago.

"I get the feeling that you're not comfortable with this assignment and only accepted it to pacify your boss. Is that why we're here? Because Mr. Watson pressured you to meet with me?"

Azure couldn't look Harper in the eye. "I told you," she said, staring down at her salad plate. "I want to profile you for the magazine."

"I know what you told me, but I don't believe you. What's really going on, Azure? Or should I call you *Alice?*"

A hand flew to her mouth, and her eyes became big brown, beautiful saucers.

"If you knew who I was all along, why didn't you say anything?"

"Why didn't you?" he countered, grinning like the Cheshire cat.

"I don't know. I guess I wanted to see if you would remember me."

"I didn't initially, but when you mentioned working at Fat Burger, something clicked in my mind. I spent a lot of time at that fast food joint, and—"

"So did I. That's why I packed on the freshman fifteen and the senior forty!"

"I thought you were cute. All hips and curves and legs." Leaning to the right, Harper raised the crisp white tablecloth and glanced under the table. "Still are."

His joke alleviated the tension, but the knot in Azure's throat remained.

"You've certainly changed a lot since Willingham Prep School." Harper stroked his jaw reflectively as he admired her appearance. Back in the day, Azure had lacked confidence, but now she carried herself with the grace of the First Lady. "What else have you been up to besides revamping your look?"

Azure filled him in. Told him about her freelance career, receiving her master's degree in communications from the University of Philadelphia and her current position at the magazine. "I've been dreaming of writing for *Eminence* ever since I saw their debut issue on newsstands in 1995. I've been a huge fan of the publication for years, and I was thrilled when they hired me last year to be a senior staff writer. I worked my butt off to get the job, but all the sacrifices I made were definitely worth it."

"You talk a lot about your career, but you haven't said anything about your personal life. You say there's no special man in your life, but I find it hard to believe a woman as captivating and as vivacious as you are isn't being bombarded with phone calls for dates."

"I could say the same thing about you. Where's *Mrs.* Harper Hamilton?"

Harper chuckled. He liked her moxie, enjoyed her wit and sense of humor. But he still hadn't figured out what Azure was after, and that frustrated him like hell. "You're not here to reminisce about our old high school days or to interview me for your magazine, are you?"

Guilt troubled her conscience. Azure wished she could forget why they were there and just enjoy Harper's company.

His gaze, suddenly dark and predatory, slid across her face and down her body. A chill vibrated along her spine. Telling Harper the real reason she'd tracked him down wasn't going to be easy, but it was the right thing to do. She'd spun her web of lies, and now it was time to tell Harper the truth, the whole truth and nothing *but* the truth. Azure started to speak, but when the waiter arrived, carrying plates and drinks and bubbling with good cheer, she closed her mouth.

"Louis wants you and your girlfriend to have a good time tonight," the waiter said, unloading his tray, "so he sent over the most popular items on our new menu."

"These bread sticks are delicious," Azure said, plucking one from the basket and taking a healthy bite. "My compliments to the chef!"

The waiter drizzled fresh basil on their entrées and after promising not to disturb them, set off for the kitchen. For the next ten minutes, they ate in silence, only speaking to comment on the taste of the food.

To buy herself some time, Azure chewed each delicious bite slowly. She needed time to think, to figure out what she was going to do next, because something told her Harper wasn't done grilling her.

"Azure, I'm waiting."

"For what?" she asked, feigning ignorance. "You better hurry up and eat before there's nothing left. These shrimp balls are slap-your-mama good, and I'm starving!"

Harper released a deep belly laugh, one that filled the dining room area. "I like having dinner with a woman who enjoys a good meal."

"What else do you like?"

"I'd like for you to come clean." Gone was the playful air, his boyish smile. "You're skilled at using humor as a diversion, but I'm skilled at uncovering the truth, and we're not leaving here tonight until you tell me what's really going on."

Azure put down her fork. Might as well since she'd lost her appetite. Her seafood pasta was moist, and the creamy Alfredo sauce flavorful, but Azure couldn't eat another bite. Her stomach was clenched into a fist, and she was sweating like a burlesque dancer in a sauna.

Folding her napkin, she dabbed at her forehead and lips. A sip of water alleviated the lump in her throat, but she was still shaking from head to toe. Azure opened her mouth, and the truth tumbled out, one embarrassing, humiliating word at a time. "My boss thought the piece I handed in on your family was crap," she confessed. "Leland said I didn't ask the right questions or dig hard enough for dirt, and according to him, dirt sells magazines by the thousands."

Harper sat quietly, without saying a word.

"Leland is convinced your family is hiding some big, dark secret, and he told me to find out what it is or else."

Anger darkened his face, but Azure saw sympathy in his eyes, a glimmer of compassion.

"A lot of writers fabricate stories to make a name for themselves...."

"I would never do that," she said, offended by what Harper was insinuating. "I'd rather admit that I failed and get fired than lie to get ahead." At the thought of telling her boss the truth, Azure broke out into a cold sweat. Leland had a temper like Chris Brown and could be as cruel as an African dictator. Azure was not looking forward to their Friday morning meeting, and wondered if she should just hand in her resignation letter and be done with it.

"Your boss would be stupid to fire you. You're very down-to-earth, and you make the people you're interviewing feel comfortable. My dad rarely talks about his childhood, but he did with you, and once you encouraged him to open up, he wouldn't stop talking!"

Azure smiled, but the heavy feeling in her chest remained.

"Leland's only been at *Eminence* for a few months, but if there's one thing I've learned about him it's that he doesn't make idle threats. Last week, he fired a pregnant staffer for insubordination and had her escorted off the premises. I'll be lucky if he lets me stay long enough to clean out my desk."

The rowdy group at the other end of the restaurant started singing "Happy Birthday," and after three rounds of boisterous applause, they began stuffing their faces with cake.

"How was everything?" the waiter asked, collecting their plates.

"Great, thanks." Azure forced a smile onto her lips.

"Would you care to see the dessert menu?"

Harper declined, and once the waiter left, he set his sights back on Azure.

"I'm sorry for wasting your time, Harper. I shouldn't have let my boss bully me into setting up a meeting with you." Uncomfortable with the blinding intensity of his gaze, she lowered her eyes to her hands and fiddled with the silver bracelet her roommate, Maggie, had given her for her birthday last month. "Tomorrow, when I get to work, I'll tell Leland there is no story."

"I appreciate you telling me the truth, Azure. I know that couldn't have been easy." His touch on her arm was light, full of tenderness and warmth, and his smile friendly. "Don't stress out about your job. I have a feeling everything will work out."

"You do?"

"What if you could give Leland the big story he's looking for?"

Azure raised her bent shoulders. What was Harper about to disclose? she wondered, studying his face for clues. A hundred scenarios raced through her head. What was the Hamilton family dynasty hiding? A financial scandal? A crooked billionaire client? A skeleton in the closet? It didn't matter. Harper had a story, something scandalous about his family he was willing to divulge, and she planned to use it to her advantage.

"I have a story that will benefit us both."

Picking up her notebook, she snatched her pen off the table. "Go ahead. I'm all ears. Start from the beginning, and go slow, because I don't want to miss anything."

Harper wore an arch grin. "Marry me."

Chapter 5

Azure felt her eyes widen, and her mouth drop open. *Marry you?* The thought was crazy. So crazy, in fact, she refused to even consider it. Either she misunderstood him or... No, no, that had to be it. Sometimes when she didn't get enough sleep her brain got fuzzy, and this proved that she needed to quit watching reality TV into the wee hours of the morning and turn in early.

"Marry me," he proposed, leaning forward in his seat, "and you'll have everything you've ever dreamed of. Fame, success, popularity."

In her haste to speak, Azure stumbled over her tongue. "Th-that's your big, juicy story? The one that's supposed to save my job and give your family more press?"

"Yeah, that's it." He nodded, looked as proud as a peacock sporting new feathers.

Azure nixed an eye roll. Harper was a true gentleman, and

the last thing she wanted to do was offend him, but he sucked at saving the day. "I need another drink. Where's the waiter?"

Harper's gaze circled the room, and when he spotted one of the male servers, he signaled him over. Harper was anxious to lay out his plan, but he waited patiently until the server refilled their glasses with water before he resumed speaking. Only Azure wouldn't let him. She held up a hand, cutting him off midword.

"Harper, I'm not interested. I love working at *Eminence* and I don't want to lose my job, but I'm not going to marry you for kicks. I don't like hurting or deceiving people, and my parents would kill me if they knew I got married for fun!"

"Really? You did a darn good job trying to trick me." The moment the words left Harper's mouth, he regretted them. A frown bruised Azure's moist red lips, and her eyes thinned into a glare. "I shouldn't have said that. I'm sorry."

"No, don't be. You're right. I haven't exactly been honest, but what you're asking me to do is unethical. Worse, this whole marriage-of-convenience thing could backfire in my face. Then I'd be humiliated, out of a job and the butt of everyone's jokes. No way, no, thanks."

"Hear me out, Azure. I promise to make this worth your while." Harper felt his excitement grow. His plan was a winner, the answer to all of his problems. To become a household name, he needed to shake things up, to think out of the box, and what better way to boost his popularity than by marrying sleek and sophisticated Azure Ellison?

Harper sneered inwardly when he remembered his conversation with his dad. His father's words played in his mind, and although he gave his head a hard shake, he couldn't break free of his thoughts. *You could learn a thing or two from Jake.... He's parlayed his engagement into a huge news story and is attracting wealthy clients left and right....*

Adrenaline surged through Harper's veins. It was the same

feeling he got whenever he stepped into a packed courtroom and delivered closing arguments. *I've got this.* All he had to do now was convince Azure, but he had the gift of persuasion, and planned to use every weapon in his arsenal to get the vivacious magazine writer on board. "This is what I propose we do—"

Azure shook her head. "Save it, Harper. I'm not interested."

"Of course you are. You want to keep your job and advance your career, don't you?"

"Yes, but not like this."

Slowly, meticulously, Harper laid out his plan. "We'll embark on a marriage of convenience but let the world think it's the real thing. A whirlwind romance between two old high school chums," he explained, his tone strong, convincing. "*Eminence* will get exclusive rights to our wedding photos, and our first interview as a married couple, as well. We'll appear at as many social engagements as possible and play up our love story for the cameras whenever we're out in public. Your boss will love you, we'll be touted in the media as the newest power couple to watch and everyone will be happy."

"What's in it for *you?*"

"Free press and a leg up on the competition."

"You mean your cousin Jake, right?"

Harper shrugged nonchalantly. "Him, too."

"When do you want to get married?" she asked, her curiosity getting the best of her.

"I'm flexible, but it would have to be soon, preferably by the end of the month."

Azure's hands were shaking, but she picked up her glass and sipped her ice water. It didn't help. Her mouth was still dry, and her body temperature was still rising fast. Another question rose in her thoughts, one that increased her anxiety and troubled her conscience. "How long are we supposed to stay hitched for?"

"Three months sounds like a reasonable amount of time."

"Three months!" Azure shrieked, drowning out the country music song playing softly in the background. "I can't pretend to be your wife for twelve weeks! I could probably handle going back and forth between your place and mine for a couple weeks, but not for three months."

"That's why I'd expect you to live with me."

"Every day?"

"And night."

Azure swallowed. Good God, he'd thought of everything. But why was she surprised? He was Harper Hamilton, one of the most successful and respected lawyers in the state, and for good reason. The man was meticulous, thorough, the type of person who never slept in or ran out of gas on the freeway, or ever missed a credit card payment.

Unlike her.

Shivering, she rubbed her chilled hands together. Azure didn't want to think about what would happen if she got fired; the possibilities were terrifying, scarier than any eighties slasher movie. With her student loans, her car payment and her ever-increasing rent, it was getting harder and harder to live the American dream. That's why Azure had to keep her job. Writing jobs were hard to come by, and after years of pounding the pavement and doing crummy freelance gigs, Azure was thrilled to be gainfully employed. And at a popular, award-winning African-American publication no less.

"This is a win-win situation for the both of us, Azure."

"Harper, this is crazy."

"Crazy-smart," he countered. "Our wedding is going to garner enormous press, but imagine what the coverage will be like once we split up?"

"Have you been talking to J-Lo's people?"

Harper chuckled. "I don't need to. I know how these things work. Divorce is big business. I should know. I'm an attorney!"

"I want to advance my career, and I'd love to be senior editor at *Eminence* one day, but I can't marry you, Harper. I'm sorry."

"You can't or you won't? I was right all along, wasn't I? There *is* someone in your life."

"That's not it."

"Are you sure?"

"Positive. Trust me. I'm as single as they come."

Harper heard the angst in her voice, the hint of sarcasm. "You sound like my assistant. She's looking for a nice, respectable guy to settle down with and—"

"A nice, respectable guy? Is there such a thing?" Azure couldn't recall the details of her last date. It had been *that* uneventful. A complete waste of time. It had been months since she went out with someone, and even longer since she'd felt a real, genuine connection.

Until now, her inner voice whispered.

"Marry me. You won't regret it." Harper gathered steam, delivered a pitch that would impress a used-car salesman. "Being Mrs. Harper Hamilton will open doors for you, and soon you'll have your pick of writing jobs. This marriage will be mutually beneficial—"

Azure cut him off. "Just what kind of benefits are you talking about?"

Another chuckle, this one louder and longer. "You have nothing to worry about, Azure. You'll be perfectly safe in my home. This is a no-strings-attached deal, and I'm not looking for a friends-with-benefits setup, either. I don't have the time."

Too bad, she thought, but didn't say. Azure scolded herself. She had to stop doing that, had to start thinking with her brain instead of her flesh. Men like Harper—ambitious, career-driven types—were obsessed with their jobs, and although Azure wasn't in the market for Mr. Right, she wanted to be with someone who'd fully commit to her.

"We'll be sleeping in separate rooms, and I won't be keeping tabs on you or anything, but while we're married, I'd expect you not to date anyone else. It wouldn't look good."

"I understand. Makes sense."

"And I'll cover all of your personal expenses while we're married," he explained, sweetening the deal. "That includes your rent, your car payment, gas, whatever. And a thousand dollar weekly stipend. What do you think?"

That I could be debt free by the end of the year! Azure considered his offer, gave it some serious thought. She'd be a fool not to accept his proposition. They didn't know each other, let alone love each other, but for some crazy, inexplicable reason, Azure wanted to marry Harper. The benefits to being Mrs. Harper Hamilton were too numerous to count.

Think about what this could do for my career!

Azure swallowed a squeal. No use letting Harper see how excited she was. She was going to marry one of the most eligible bachelors in Philadelphia—a strong, virile man who every woman wanted, and every man wanted to be—and his name and connections were going to increase her celebrity. And who wouldn't love that? *If I play my cards right, this marriage-of-convenience gig could catapult me straight into the editor's chair at* Eminence *magazine!*

"I think I covered everything," Harper said, his eyes narrowed in concentration. "Do you have any more questions or is the plan crystal clear?"

"Oh, it's clear, all right. You want us to get married, pretend to be madly in love to garner good press then break up three months later so you can get sympathy press."

"I won't make you out to be the bad guy, Azure. Trust me. We'll both come out on top."

He sounded sincere, convincing, but that was no surprise. He *was* an attorney. One of the best in the business. And so damn suave and debonair the women seated in the booth beside them had been stealing long, lusty looks at him all night.

"So, are you in or do I have to find myself another trophy wife?"

Biting down on her bottom lip, she thought long and hard about his outlandish proposal. Her mind was screaming, *No, don't do it,* but her mouth didn't receive the message, and when the word "Yes" sprang out of her lips, it surprised them both.

"Yes, as in you'll marry me?"

Nodding her head, like a puppet on a string, she grabbed her cocktail glass and downed the rest of her drink. The cold, sweet liquid relaxed her, eased her stress. "I'll do it, but you're going to have your work cut out for you, Harper. Anyone who knows me knows I think marriage is outdated and unnecessary and—"

"Unnecessary?"

"Yes, unnecessary," she repeated, prepared to defend her opinion. "Back in the day women married to have children, to help their parents financially or because they were pressured to, but today sisters are handling their business. They're parenting alone, skyrocketing up the corporate ladder, making a killing on the stock market and looking damn good doing it, too!"

"I agree. Couldn't have said it better myself, actually."

"Really?"

Harper nodded. "I definitely don't have the marriage chip, and—"

"The what?"

"The marriage chip," he repeated, in all seriousness. "Some

men are programmed to marry, and some aren't. Like me. I just don't have it in me to make a lifelong commitment, and I don't see that changing anytime soon."

"Great. I think marriage is antiquated, and you're a commitment-phobe," Azure quipped, shaking her head. "This publicity stunt is doomed to fail. None of my friends will ever believe you swept me off my feet or that we're madly in love."

"They will." His tone was firm, filled with resolve and determination. "I guarantee it."

"You guarantee it? How can you be so confident?"

Harper's gaze was intense, and his smile packed one hell of a punch. "I convinced *you* to marry me, didn't I?"

Chapter 6

"Ellison, where the hell have you been? I've been looking all over for you!"

Azure froze—hands, legs, erratically beating heart. Berating herself for her lack of self-control, she abandoned her search for sugar cubes in the staff room cupboards and faced her temperamental boss, who was standing in front of the door like a five-foot-five human barricade.

Sighing inwardly, Azure pushed a hand nervously through her hair. This was what she got for leaving her office. Feeling sluggish, and needing a midmorning caffeine fix, she'd quit writing her latest article and headed straight for the staff room. Now she was paying the price for being addicted to coffee.

Feeding her boss a smile, Azure picked up her steaming mug of java from off the wooden table and sipped her latte. Sure, the freshly brewed coffee tasted divine and warmed her chilled body, but it wasn't worth being reamed out by her boss in the deserted staff room.

"Where have you been?" he repeated, spitting out the words in his thick New Jersey accent. "Been waiting for you to put in an appearance all morning."

"I was in my office finishing up my latest proposal."

His eyes were full of judgment and scorn. "Dig up any dirt on the Hamiltons yet?"

"No, but I'm working on it."

"You're not working fast enough," Leland snapped, folding his scrawny arms. Her boss was a chain smoker, who'd rather drink coffee than eat, and every time he scowled his pale, hollow cheeks caved in. "Set up another meeting with Harper. And fast."

"I already did. We're having dinner again tonight."

Leland raised a fuzzy eyebrow. "I heard you two looked awfully cozy last night at that quaint little steak house on Sixth Street."

Azure opened her mouth to ask how he knew they had dined at the out-of-the-way restaurant, but thought better of it. Leland wouldn't tell her. Her boss had more spies than the CIA and spent most of his day behind his desk, whispering into his cell phone. "Men like Harper Hamilton aren't easily fooled," he began, his voice taking on a grave tone, "so to gain his trust you'll have to use the Delilah method."

"The Delilah method?" Azure repeated, frowning. "What's that?"

"The key to getting close to Harper. That little vixen Delilah used persuasion and seduction to trick Samson, and those tactics still work today. Just ask any local politician!"

Leland snorted like a potbellied pig playing in a fresh pool of mud.

Azure was disgusted but wore a blank expression on her face. Knowing what she was about to say would pique Leland's interest gave her great satisfaction, so Azure spoke slowly, drawing out every word to maximize the effect. "I don't need to use tricks to earn Harper's trust," she said, her lips overwhelmed by a smile. "We really hit it off last night, and—"

"Is he interested in you romantically?"

Azure gave a nervous laugh. "I don't know."

"Of course you do," he insisted, crossing his arms. "A woman *always* knows."

"Oh wow, look at the time," Azure said, gesturing to the wall clock above the door. "I better get back to my office. Harper promised to call me at noon, and I'd hate to miss his call."

Leland pointed a bony finger at her. "I'm giving you until the end of this week to dig up some dirt on the Hamilton family, and not a day more. If you can't give me what I'm looking for, I'll find someone else who will."

Then he strode out of the staff room and out of sight.

Azure was glad to see him go. Back in her cubicle, she took her tape recorder out of her purse, put in her earpiece and hit Play. When she heard Harper's deep, masculine voice, a sigh escaped her lips. Azure told herself she had to listen to the interview to make notes, but it was a lie. She'd listened to the recording last night in bed, that morning while she was getting ready for work and again on the train. She couldn't get enough of his voice, couldn't get enough of the feelings and sensations his words evoked.

"I'm proud of the work my family's done for the Tuck Me In Foundation," Harper said, the pride in his voice shining through, "and this year we're hoping to raise a million dollars for children in foster care."

Azure liked that Harper wasn't like the other guys she'd met from rich families who thought they owned the world. He cared about people, especially neglected children, and had a heart of gold. Harper Hamilton was one hell of a gorgeous man, too, and for the next three months, he was all hers.

Her office phone rang, so loud it drowned out Harper's rich, soothing tone. Azure pulled her earpiece out with one hand and snatched up the receiver with the other. "Good morning. Azure Ellison speaking."

"Alice, I'm so glad I finally reached you! I've been ringing you all week, but with no success."

Azure slumped back in her swivel chair. She couldn't remember the last time she'd spoken to her parents, but when she heard her mother's voice, her good mood evaporated. And every time her mother called her by her given name, she remembered the cruel taunts of her middle school classmates. "Hi, Mom," she said, feigning excitement. "How are you and Dad doing? Everything okay?"

"We're fine, honey. Your dad's out playing golf with some friends, and I'm on my way to a Botox party, so I can't talk long."

Azure shook her head. Her mother was never going to change. Against aging gracefully, she tried everything under the sun to keep wrinkles at bay. It didn't matter how much it cost, her mother gave it a try. And more often than not, it made things worse, not better.

"How far is your place from the airport?"

"About an hour. Why?"

"Your sister has a layover in Philly, and I thought she could spend the night at your place, but you're much too far and I'd hate for her to miss her six o'clock flight the next morning."

Azure wondered why Eden hadn't called her directly, but decided not to make an issue of it. She and her younger sister had never been close, and they only spoke during the holidays. Azure had been jealous of her sister since they were kids and envied the close, loving relationship Eden had with their mom. To avoid feeling like the third wheel, Azure visited her parents when she knew her sister wouldn't be around, and she never asked her mom about Eden's modeling gigs.

"There are a lot of really great hotels near the airport," she said, taking her planner out of her purse and flipping it open to October. "If you know what day Eden's coming in, I can book a suite for her at the Hyatt."

"She's arriving on October twenty-fifth at seven in the evening."

"I'll make the arrangements and text it to her by the end of the day."

"That would be perfect, honey. Thanks a bunch," her mother said, her tone bright and cheery. "Did you get the email I sent you?"

"Which one?" Azure grumbled, tapping her ball-point pen on her computer keyboard. Every week, without fail, her mother sent her an exhaustive list of diet tips and interval-training routines that would cause a participant on *Celebrity Fit Club* to go into cardiac arrest.

"The recipes are nutritious and tasty and real easy to make."

Hell no, and no, thanks, Azure decided, remembering the vegan recipes her mother had emailed days earlier. *I'd rather die chubby and full than thin and hungry.*

"I've only been on the green bean diet for a week, but I've already lost three pounds!"

"That's great, Mom. Good for you."

"What would be great is if you took your health a little more seriously."

"Not everyone can be a size six like you, Mom."

"Honey, please, I've never been *that* fat. I'm a slim and trim size four."

Azure didn't want to argue with her image-obsessed mother about her weight, but she had to set her straight. Again. Every time they spoke, her mom put her down, and

Azure was tired of having to defend herself and her body. "I eat well, I exercise several times a week and I hardly drink alcohol."

Unless I'm on a date with Harper Hamilton and I need a cosmopolitan or two or three to help calm my nerves.

"I didn't want to say anything when you came down to visit for Labor Day, but you have love handles, Alice, and they're most unflattering."

Only her family still called her Alice, her given name. Pushing her chair away from her desk, she stared down at her hips. *What love handles?*

"You career will never take off if you keep putting on weight, and if you're not careful, you'll lose your job altogether," she stated, her tone matter-of-fact. "I'll ask Eden to show you some of her workout routines when she comes to town. Your sister's in talks to be in the Victoria's Secret holiday fashion show and she's been working her butt off to get in tip-top shape. Eden looks better than ever, and I bet she wouldn't mind showing you some of her tricks."

Azure's good mood fizzled and died, and when her mother encouraged her to try the Master Cleanse for thirty days, the knot in her chest threatened to choke her. *Will I ever be good enough?* she wondered, overcome with sadness.

Azure was relieved when her mother ended the conversation seconds later to head off to her Botox party, but long after Azure hung up the phone, she could still hear her mother's words playing in her mind. *First, I get reamed out from my boss, and then my mother bashes my body. Hell of a way to start the day,* she thought sourly, tossing her pen down on the desk.

The telephone buzzed. And when Azure saw the editorial director's name pop up on the screen, she knew her day had taken another turn for the worse, because the only time her director called was when there was a problem.

Hands shaking, mouth dry, Azure picked up the receiver and greeted the South African–born mother of two warmly. The news was worse than bad, and when Azure hung up the phone twenty minutes later, the tears in her eyes broke free.

"You're never going to believe this," Maggie Sharpe said, busting into the living room of the two-bedroom condo she shared with Azure and dumping her shopping bags at her feet. "Guess who eloped to Cancún?"

From the floor where she was exercising, Azure stared at her roommate, and for the second time that week wondered what Maggie was thinking when she got dressed. The high school drama teacher had a fabulously curvy figure, but instead of wearing flattering pieces that enhanced her bootylicious assets, she hid her plus-size shape in peasant dresses and bulky blazers. Her makeup was flawless, but her cheeks were flushed and it looked as if a toddler had been playing in her blond-streaked hair. "I don't know," Azure replied, rolling onto her back. "One of the *Jersey Shore* kids?"

Maggie rolled her eyes. "No, silly, it's someone we know."

"Beats me. Most of my friends are either dating or unhappily married."

"Do you remember my cousin Danity?"

"No."

"Of course you do." Maggie put her cell phone down on the coffee table, then plopped on the love seat and folded her short, plump legs under her butt. "We ran into her a couple months ago at that fusion club on a hundred and twenty-first Street. She has ridiculously long hair and a gorgeous, surgically enhanced body."

Azure nodded. How could she forget Maggie's politically incorrect cousin who'd flirted with everyone from the bouncer to the bartender? "Yeah, I remember her," Azure said, as bits and pieces of that night resurfaced in her mind. "She's got quite the personality."

"Well, her sister, Sienna, just eloped with some dude she met online. Isn't that insane?"

"Maybe it was love at first sight."

"More like lust at first sight. They've only known each other for six weeks!"

You think that's fast? Azure thought. *I've got her beat by almost a whole month!* Thinking about her own shot-gun wedding in the works reminded Azure about the article she'd turned in yesterday. The one her editorial director hated and insisted she rewrite. Azure scowled, shook her head. A month's worth of research and five days of writing down the drain. And if she wanted to meet her Thursday morning dead-line, she'd have to skip tonight's *Dancing With the Stars* and pull an all-nighter. "You're right, Maggie, six weeks isn't a lot of time to get to know someone, but I recently interviewed couples who got hitched twenty-four hours after meeting, and they're all still going strong."

"Wow" tumbled out of Maggie's mouth. "Kardashians don't even get married that fast."

"I guess when you know, you know," Azure said, using her white cotton towel to clean the sweat off her face and neck. "Or at least that's what I've been told."

"I'd never do something that impulsive. I want to get mar-ried once. *Not* once a year."

Azure opened her mouth, then quickly closed it. She wanted to tell Maggie about her meeting with Harper last night, but sensed now was not the right time. Not after what her roommate had just said. The funny thing was, Azure agreed with Maggie. Marriage wasn't something to be en-tered into lightly, and although she'd agreed to marry Harper at the end of the month, she was having a serious case of buyer's remorse. The truth was, Azure was attracted to him, which in the end had made her easy prey. He'd worked his magic on her, one boyish grin and smoldering gaze at a time. Harper wouldn't take no for an answer. Like with the rest of the Hamilton clan, the word didn't exist in his vocabulary, and sadly, she'd been no match for the suave, persuasive attorney with the bedroom eyes.

Last night, they'd sat at their secluded corner table drinking, talking and laughing for hours. If not for the restaurant closing, they probably would have stayed there all night. After paying their bill, Harper walked her to her car and helped her slip inside the driver's seat. His rich, wonderful cologne settled over her, and when he leaned in for a hug, Azure brushed her lips across his cheek. Hoping he'd take the hint, she waited anxiously for him to kiss her. It never happened. Instead of taking her right then and there in the front seat, he promised to be in touch, closed the driver's-side door and strode off. Azure couldn't remember the last time she'd been so bummed. Twenty-four hours later, she was still thinking about what could have been. One thing was for sure, though— she had to smarten up. Harper was only pretending to love her; it was not the real thing. And as long as she remembered that, she'd come out on top.

"Will you come?"

Azure blinked. She'd been so busy thinking about Harper, and the kiss that didn't happen, she'd missed what her roommate said. "Of course I'll come," she replied, matching her friend's enthusiasm. Azure wondered if she'd just agreed to attend a play at the high school Maggie taught at or a gallery opening. Either one would bore her to death.

"Great!" Maggie beamed. "Is Friday night good for you?"

I should probably check with my fiancé. It was an absurd thought, but she'd agreed to marry Harper, and until he changed his mind, that's exactly what he was—her fiancé. "I'll have to get back to you—"

The doorbell rang.

Panic flashed in Maggie's eyes. "Oh no, Greg's an hour early! Roomy, keep him company while I get changed." Swiping her shopping bags off the floor, she shot up the stairs faster than a gold-medal-winning track star and disappeared down the hallway.

Glad she'd taken the time to clean up before working out, Azure smiled in satisfaction as she glanced around. It had been her idea to decorate in white, and although it was impossible to keep the condo clean, she loved the fresh, modern look it gave her home. Vases overflowing with bamboo stalks stood in each corner of the room, vintage paintings lined the teal walls, and the cinnamon candles filled the air with a rich, intoxicating scent. The open-concept design was perfect for entertaining, and the tall windows ushered in streams of natural sunlight.

The doorbell buzzed again. And again.

Azure grabbed her water bottle and guzzled down the rest of her drink as she dragged her weary body into the foyer. She opened the door, fully prepared to tease Maggie's boyfriend for ringing the doorbell like a maniac, but when Azure saw who the caller was the rebuke died on her parted lips. Her knees buckled, and she struggled to stay upright. Azure wanted to rub her eyes but didn't. She wasn't seeing things, wasn't hallucinating like a character in a paranormal movie. Harper was here. For real. Standing on her doorstep, looking all *GQ* in a black tailored suit and an eye-catching striped tie, he wore a rich smile that only enhanced his killer sex appeal.

"Honey, I'm home."

Harper chuckled, but Azure didn't. There was nothing to hee-haw about. She was wearing tiny booty shorts, not a stroke of makeup and she reeked of sweat. Not a pleasant combination, and when Harper raised his thick, trimmed eyebrows, Azure wondered if it was because her hair was a wild, frizzy mess or because her post-workout look was frightening.

"What are you doing here?" she asked tightly.

"I came here to discuss our wedding plans."

"You could have called."

"Yes, but then I wouldn't have been able to see you." He sounded sincere, as heartfelt as a lawyer could be. "Besides, we have a lot to discuss, and a ten-minute conversation on the phone wouldn't suffice."

"How did you find me?"

"You're in the phone book."

Azure winced. Duh. *That* was a stupid question. "We went over everything last night during dinner. What else is there to discuss? We're getting married at the end of the month, at the courthouse, at noon. Don't worry, I'll be there."

"There's been a slight change of plans."

"Why? I like the plan we already have."

Harper tried to keep his eyes on her face, but his gaze kept sliding down to her bare midriff. Her T-shirt said Kiss My Abs, and her spandex shorts were so small they could double as a handkerchief. Azure was still all arms and hips and legs, and when he caught sight of her cleavage, he lost the use of his tongue. Clearing his throat, he hoped he didn't look as foolish as he felt. "Can I come in?" he asked, forcing the words up his throat and out of his dry mouth.

"Here? Now?"

"Is this a bad time?"

Azure replied with a nod. "Yeah, I just finished my workout, and I was about to go take a long shower."

"Do you have plans tonight?"

"I have an article to write."

"Can I persuade you to have dinner with me?" he asked, lowering his voice to a soft, silky hue. "After we eat, we can choose a venue and discuss the wedding ceremony."

"Sorry to keep you waiting, Greg. I couldn't find my—"

At the sound of her roommate's voice, Azure stiffened. Her body shut down, and for several long seconds, she couldn't move.

"Sorry," Maggie said, wearing a sheepish smile. "I thought you were my boyfriend."

"We all can't be that lucky, now, can we?" Harper replied.

A giggle tumbled out of her mouth. "No, I guess not."

"You must be Azure's roommate. Maggie, right?"

"Yeah, and you are…"

"Harper Hamilton." He stepped forward and shut the door skillfully with the back of his right foot. Azure stood there, dumbfounded. *Guess we're staying in,* she thought miserably, bolting the lock. As Azure turned toward the living room, she caught a whiff of her T-shirt and wrinkled her nose. *I smell so bad I could kill a skunk!* A shower was just what the doctor ordered, but Azure didn't want to leave Harper alone with Maggie. No way. No how. Her roommate knew too many of her embarrassing secrets and unfortunately had the gift of gab.

"It's wonderful to finally meet you, Maggie," Harper said smoothly. "Azure's told me a lot about you."

"She has? I'm surprised. She hasn't mentioned you once."

Harper rested a hand on Azure's shoulder. He tenderly stroked her neck, and when she stared up at him, all bright-eyed and surprised, he nuzzled his face playfully against her ear. "That's to be expected," he said smoothly. "We haven't been dating long."

Maggie's vivid blue eyes were the size of baseballs. "S-so, you're her boyfriend?"

"That's right, and proud of it. I've waited my whole life to meet a woman like Azure, and now that I've found her, I'm never going to let her go." Then Harper bent down, cupped her chin and pressed his mouth softly against hers. His lips tasted like peppermint, and his refreshing, citrus scent wrapped itself around her in a sensual embrace.

Before Azure knew what was happening, the kiss was over.

"Azure!" Maggie whispered, speaking out the side of her mouth, just loud enough for Azure to hear. "Why would you agree to go on a blind date with my school janitor if you were seeing someone? And not just anyone. You're dating Harper frickin' Hamilton! I want details, roomy, and I want them now!"

Azure's head was spinning. Still reeling from Harper's kiss, she tried to make sense of what her roommate had just said. Tilting her head to the right, she squinted, thought hard for a minute. She didn't remember agreeing to go out with anyone, let alone a high school janitor. Seconds passed. Then recognition dawned. *It must have been earlier when Maggie was talking, and I was zoned out,* Azure decided, glad she'd cracked the mystery. *I guess that's what I get for daydreaming about Harper.* "I'll explain later," Azure whispered back.

"You better, or else."

"This is a great condo," Harper said, glancing around the spacious main floor. "Cool décor, and I love all the framed movie posters."

Azure started to speak, but Maggie cut her off.

"How did you guys meet?" she asked, directing the question at Harper. "My roommate's been keeping me in the dark, but I'm dying to know how you two hooked up."

Harper lowered his hand to Azure's waist and held her close to his side, as if to prevent her from running away. "We went to prep school together, but lost touch after graduation. Azure interviewed my family for *Eminence* last month and when she walked into my uncle's estate, I instantly recognized her. We've been inseparable ever since."

"You have?"

Azure's heart flip-flopped in her chest. Harper was staring at her with such longing, with such adoration, Azure almost forgot that this was all part of the plan. She found herself falling under his spell, believing every word that came out of his mouth, and she could tell by the love-struck expression on Maggie's face that she was eating it up, too.

"I'm going to go change," Azure said, hoping the sound of her voice would snap her roommate out of her haze.

It didn't. Maggie continued staring at Harper, and when her pink, rhinestone-studded cell phone buzzed, she made no moves to answer it.

"That's probably Greg." Azure snatched her roommate's iPhone off the glass coffee table and handed it to her. "Here. Answer it."

Maggie flapped her hands in the air like a bald eagle taking flight. "We have company, Azure. That would be rude." Smiling at Harper, her baby blues shimmering with delight, she offered him a drink. "What can I get you? Water? Coffee? A Heineken, maybe?"

"I'd love one."

"Go ahead and freshen up, roomy. I'll keep Harper company while you're gone."

"I bet you will," Azure grumbled, giving her roommate the evil eye.

Chapter 7

"I haven't crammed this hard since I took my SATs!" Azure said, massaging her throbbing temples. Since they sat down at the kitchen table with their containers of Greek takeout, Harper had been filling her in on his childhood, his hobbies and his day-to-day life, and Azure, the dutiful student, had been taking precise notes. "I never imagined pulling off a publicity stunt like this would require so much work."

"And we still have a lot of ground to cover," Harper said, consulting the to-do list he'd made that afternoon. "I haven't given you the backstory on my brothers yet, and there are some relatives in town I need to tell you about, as well."

"I know we've only been at this for an hour, but I'm beat!"

Chuckling, Harper reached out, took her hand in his and gave it an affectionate squeeze. "You're doing great, Azure, and after we finish up with this I promise to get out of your hair. I know you have an article to write, and I've already taken up enough of your time."

Azure couldn't speak. His touch had rendered her speech-less, and Azure feared if she opened her mouth she'd babble like a six-month-old baby. Needing a moment to gather herself, she stared down at her iPad and carefully reviewed the information she'd jotted down about Harper. He was passion-ate about giving back to the community, loved Greek cui-sine and played basketball every second Saturday with his brothers and cousins at his uncle's estate, Integrity. Azure knew Harper's likes and dislikes, and everything in between, and found herself hanging on to every word that came out of his delicious-looking mouth.

"One last thing about my parents. My mom will invite you to call her by her first name, but don't," he advised. "Always address her as Mrs. Hamilton, and my father, too."

"Got it. No cute names for the in-laws." Recalling that Mrs. Hamilton had been absent from the interview she did last month at his uncle's Integrity estate, Azure questioned Harper about his mother's thriving business. "Your mom's fall collection had received rave reviews from fashion in-dustry experts, so I'm guessing she's probably insanely busy these days. Do you see her much, or is she out of town a lot?"

"My mom has always put family first, but ever since she worked on the *Sex and the City 2* movie, her phone has been ringing off the hook. She's ditched us for Hollywood. Sad, huh?"

He gave a hearty chuckle, one that brought a smile to Azure's lips. Azure loved his laugh. Loved how rich and full it was, and how his eyes twinkled when he was amused.

"I'm proud of my mom, and I'm happy that her clothing line is such a hit. It's time she lived her dream and poured her passion and energy into doing what she loves."

"How did your parents meet?"

"Friends introduced them. My mom said the only thing she

liked about my dad was his Porsche, and Dad said he fell in love with Mom the first time he tasted her gumbo!"

Laughing, Azure made a note on her file. "I think I got everything. Anything else?"

"No, that's all for now. I don't want to overwhelm you."

"It's too late for that!"

Harper chuckled.

"Well, I know what I'll be doing this weekend," Azure quipped, tapping a finger on her iPad. "Memorizing my notes on Harper 101."

"About that," he began, straightening in his chair. "As I said before, there's been a slight change of plans."

"Oh, okay, what is it? Changed your mind about having the ceremony at the Fountain?"

"No. We're going to get hitched on October ninth."

Azure's lips parted and a shriek flew out. "October ninth?" she repeated, in a shrill, high-pitched voice she didn't recognize. "But that's in three days!"

"I know, but my mom returns from New York tomorrow morning, only to leave again at the end of the week for Paris. She's hard at work promoting her latest collection, so there's no telling how long she'll be gone. And if I get married while she's away, she'll kill me, and I have a lot of living left to do!"

Azure sat there, fidgeting with her utensils, staring off into space.

"I've already applied for our wedding license, and as long as there isn't a backlog at the magistrate's office, it should be issued within the next forty-eight hours."

"Harper, are you sure about all this? I've done a lot of impulsive things in my life, but I've never done anything *this* crazy."

"I'm sure. Don't worry. I'll take care of everything. Tomorrow, we'll meet with the event planner at the Fountain, and after we select the menu, you'll go shopping for your wedding gown. And don't worry about your expenses. I'll cover everything. Your dress, your shoes and anything else you need for our big day."

Azure gulped. Things were happening too fast.

"You have a great sense of fashion, and I hope what I'm about to say doesn't offend you, but *please* don't buy a long, poufy wedding dress." He added, "And no lace. It's old-fashioned."

"Okay, *Mr.* Fashionista," she teased, trying to keep a straight face but failing miserably, "what do you think I should wear?"

"Something sleek and sophisticated and timeless," he told her, his voice strong and earnest. "I want you to wow me, Azure. Knock my socks off."

"I think I can do that."

"Oh, I know you can."

Something about his tone aroused her. His eyes moved slowly over her scalding-hot flesh, and his broad, megawatt smile thrilled her.

"We have to keep our wedding plans a secret from our friends and family if we want maximum publicity and exposure," Harper said.

Azure frowned. "How are we going to get everyone to the Fountain without tipping them off?"

Harper thought a moment. "I'll call a family meeting. That should work."

"I'm not sure what I'll tell my boss, and Maggie, but I'll think of something between now and then."

"What about your parents?"

Azure shrugged, and didn't bother offering an excuse for why she wasn't going to invite her mom and dad. The less her parents knew about her arrangement with Harper, the better. If her mother knew she was marrying for fun, to save her job and garner free publicity, she'd be livid. Not because it was morally wrong, but because she hadn't been the one to plan and execute *her* dream wedding.

"I'll make sure your boss has a seat right out front. That should make him happy."

"I doubt it," Azure quipped, making a face. "Just make sure there's a lot of free booze!"

The pair chuckled.

"Have you ever been engaged?" Harper asked, eying her over the rim of his wineglass. "Any old fiancés or bitter, scorned lovers I need to know about?"

"Nope, never. I'm antimarriage, remember? What about you?"

"I'm wedded to my career, remember?"

Azure stuck out her tongue. "Smart-ass."

Harper belted out a laugh. "And I thought you were still that quiet, painfully shy girl who wouldn't give me the time of day in high school."

"Oh, is that the story you plan to tell your family? That I rejected you when we were in Willingham Prep, and you captured my heart the second time around?"

"Definitely." Grinning, his eyes bright with mischief, he gave a firm nod of his head. "Everyone loves an underdog, and my story will get me the sympathy vote, and—"

"Even more female attention than you're getting now!" Azure poked his shoulder. "That's not fair. When you dump me, you'll have your choice of any woman you want, and I'll be stuck fighting off the same crazy, loudmouth Philly guys."

His expression turned serious, somber, as if he were about to deliver the eulogy at his best friend's funeral. "I've never been a player, Azure. I don't have it in me to hurt or mistreat women, and my last relationship ended because *she* cheated, not me."

"That must have been hard."

"Not for the reasons you think. I liked her, but I wasn't

madly in love or anything." Harper thrust his chin forward, straightened his shoulders. "I was more embarrassed about being cheated on than anything else."

Curiosity pushed Azure to ask the question, "Did you catch her in the act?"

"No, nothing that scandalous happened."

Harper took a gulp of wine. "She was in L.A. on business, so I flew in on Valentine's Day to surprise her. I showed up to the album release party her record company was throwing, with flowers and candy, and I found her..." He stumbled over his words, then cleared his throat. "I found her in the VIP section, wasted, topless and hanging all over one of the label's hit rappers."

Azure studied Harper closely. His face looked as hard as stone, and anger crimped the corners of his mouth. "Did you confront her?"

"I made sure she saw me. That was enough."

"How long has it been since you broke up?"

"A while."

"Did your parents like her?"

"My dad did, but my mom didn't think her motives were pure. It turned out she was right. My ex was a club hopper, masquerading as the girl next door, and I'm better off without her."

Azure had a lot more questions about his ex, but instead of interrogating him like a felon on the witness stand, she said, "Your friends and family are going to think I'm a rebound."

"I don't care what they think," he snapped, a hard edge in his tone. "I'm going to milk our wedding publicity for all it's worth, and use my newfound fame to take my career to the next level. Soon, everyone in this city will know who Harper Hamilton is."

"Won't your parents be disappointed when they discover our marriage was a sham?"

"I'm not going to tell them, are you?"

"No, of course not."

"Speaking of parents, do you have any pictures of yours around? I'm curious to see what my in-laws-to-be look like."

Azure laughed. "You're taking this phony marriage thing a little too seriously."

"Anything worth doing is worth doing well," he said, his tone smooth, self-assured. "I want everyone at our wedding to believe we're hopelessly and desperately in love, and to do that, I need to know as much as possible about you and your family."

"Fair enough."

Standing, Azure cleared the kitchen table of their food containers and cutlery. Seconds later, she returned, carrying an armload of photo albums. She placed them in front of Harper, and when he opened the largest one and began flipping through pictures taken when she was a plump, pimply-faced teen, shame infected Azure's body.

"You've lost weight, but you really haven't changed all that much since high school."

"You're kidding, right? I look completely different!"

"No, you don't. You still have the same gorgeous, almond-shaped eyes, and the prettiest, brightest smile I have ever seen in my life."

Azure didn't touch his comment, but inside she was doing the happy dance. Another compliment. That was the third one tonight, and they hadn't even had dessert yet. "I wish *The Biggest Loser* had been around when I was in high school, because a complete makeover is exactly what I needed. I had no friends, and since no one asked me to the prom, my mom forced me to attend a Weight Watchers meeting."

"Don't worry, Azure, you didn't miss anything. Prom was boring and uneventful."

"It still would have been nice to go. I dreamed of wearing

the perfect dress, a pretty pink corsage and slow-dancing to 'N Sync, and not going was a huge letdown."

"At least your friends didn't secretly record you getting busy with your date."

Azure touched a hand to her mouth. "No way! They didn't!"

"Yup, and they showed the video to my brothers. Striking out was humiliating enough without having an audience, and my brothers still rib me about it to this day!"

Trading jokes and swapping embarrassing tales from their high school days made Azure feel closer to Harper and made her realize she wasn't the only one who'd had it rough at Willingham Prep. Azure matched Harper quip for quip, and by the time she served the cupcakes and ice cream for dessert, her jaw ached from laughing. She still had some serious reservations about their marriage of convenience, but sharing her doubts with Harper made Azure feel better. As Harper said, it was a win-win for the both of them, a publicity stunt for the ages, one that was guaranteed to bolster both of their careers.

"I never knew you had a sister," Harper said, staring quizzically at the photograph in front of him. "Are you older?"

Nodding, Azure helped herself to a cupcake and took a healthy bite. "I'm five years older than Eden. She's been modeling in Europe since she was a teenager, and since her husband hates the States, they only visit at Christmastime."

Thinking about Eden and her glamorous, jet-setting life made Azure feel a twinge of envy. It always did. She loved working for *Eminence* magazine, and had dreamed of being a writer since she was a child, but she'd gladly trade places with her sister. Eden and Renault traveled to fabulous places, stayed at the best hotels and had a storybook marriage filled with love, romance and enough passion for all of the disgruntled couples who aired their dirty laundry on Dr. Phil.

"You two could pass for twins."

Azure scoffed. "Right, and I'm going to be in the Victoria's Secret holiday show!"

"I'm serious. Your sister has lighter hair and she's a few inches taller than you, but aside from that you look identical—" Harper broke off speaking, watched Azure's face crumble and her temperament change right before his very eyes. "Did I say something wrong?"

Shaking her head, she softly cleared her throat. "No, it's just that no one's ever compared me to Eden before, and your words took me by surprise."

"They shouldn't. I'm telling the truth."

Concern touched his features, and his expression was one of compassion.

"I take it you and your sister don't get along."

"Growing up, Eden was always the gorgeous, glamorous girl everyone fawned over, and I was the smart one who was ridiculed and teased," Azure explained, pushing her spoon around her ice cream bowl. "My mom put me on dozens of fad diets, but the more I tried to lose weight, the more I gained. I don't blame her for being hard on me, though. I was a hot mess back then."

Harper slammed the album shut.

Azure stared at him, eyebrows raised, and when he reached out and took her hand, she felt a charge, a dizzying rush of pleasure, an invisible spark that couldn't be seen, only felt.

"I don't ever want to hear you put yourself down like that, Azure. It's hard to take."

"But it's the truth."

"It couldn't be. I knew you back in the day. You were quiet, but kind, and your smile was a thing of beauty. Still is." His eyes bore into her, moved over her flesh like an intimate caress. "I look forward to meeting your parents so I can tell them they raised the smartest, most vivacious woman I have ever had the pleasure of meeting."

A smile overwhelmed Azure's mouth and exploded across her face.

"Do your parents live in Philly?"

"Nope. They're happily retired and living in Florida."

"Will I get to meet them the next time they're in town?"

Her smile morphed into a smirk. "Sure, right after we have a couple of fake kids."

"Are you always this sarcastic?" Harper asked, enjoying their verbal sparring match. Azure laughed at all of his jokes—even the bad ones—and she was so chill, so easy to be around, he didn't want the night to end. "I have a feeling I'm going to have my hands full with you."

"It's not too late for you to find another trophy wife, you know...." Azure trailed off, pointed her spoon at the oversize wall clock above the flat-screen TV. "Table 13 is filled with debutantes and socialites every night of the week, and oh, look, it's almost happy hour...."

"I don't want anyone else but you."

Her stomach flip-flopped, churned with fear and apprehension. Azure didn't know if she could go through with their bogus wedding. It was all too much. The teasing, the flirting, Harper's blinding, megawatt smile. *If I can't make it through a single meal without getting hot and bothered, how the hell am I going to survive living with him for three months?* "I—I—I know I agreed to marry you," she began, the truth gushing out of her mouth, "but I don't think I can go through with this. You're right, Harper. I *am* a handful."

His grin widened. "I'm not worried."

"But I'm sarcastic and stubborn, and I'm a horrible cook. My ex said my spaghetti Bolognese was so dry and overcooked the homeless wouldn't eat it!"

Harper cracked up. "I just love your sense of humor."

"That's just it. I'm not kidding. That's what he said. Word for word."

He laughed some more.

"I think you'll make a great trophy wife and be a nice addition to the Hamilton family, as well. You're fun and saucy and you're not afraid to speak your mind. And we have a lot in common. You said so yourself."

Azure silently agreed. He was right. She did say that. And unfortunately, it was true. They were both hard workers, devoted to their careers and families, and die-hard Lauryn Hill fans. If they had any more in common they'd be Siamese twins.

"And besides, it's not like we're marrying for love," Harper said. He snapped his fingers. "Three months will go by like that, and before you know it, you'll be back at your apartment, hanging out with Maggie and cooking your tasty spaghetti Bolognese!"

Azure rolled her eyes to the ceiling. "Ha, ha, you're a riot. You should take your show on the road, Mr. Funny Pants."

Harper chuckled. And soon, she was laughing, too.

"Is there anything else I should know about you?"

The warmth of his gaze and the richness of his voice made Azure feel woozy, as if she'd drunk a slew of apple martinis. She took in some air, waited a moment for her thoughts to clear and her raging body heat to simmer. "Let me see," she began, giving serious consideration to the question. "I love all things celebrity, I'm addicted to cupcakes and as long as you don't expect me to be Florida Evans and pick up after you twenty-four-seven, we should get along fine!"

His touch on her hand was reassuring. "Azure, you'll be my wife in name only. I don't expect you to do anything but look great on my arm, smile for the cameras and gush about how wonderful married life is during interviews. Think you can do that?"

"The jury's still out on that one, but I'm willing to give it a try."

"That's more than enough for me."

Azure ignored her doubts, and the heavy feeling in her heart. Harper was right. They'd get married, bask in the limelight for several months and then move on. She only hoped that her heart stayed out of the picture, because the last time she'd made the mistake of falling head over heels for a wealthy, attractive man, he'd shattered her heart in two. Six months later, she was still trying to recover. Something told Azure what she and Harper were about to do was wrong—so very, very wrong—but she ignored her conscience. Harper's name and connections would open a lot of doors for her. That's why she'd accepted his outrageous proposal.

That's not the only reason, a high-pitched, female voice jeered inside her head. *You've been dreaming of kissing that man since the tenth grade!*

Azure ignored the voice, deleted the accusation from her mind. This wasn't about those silly, teenage fantasies she used to have about Harper or the blinding sexual chemistry they shared, either. This was about her career, about Azure finally beating her boss at his own game. It was her time to shine, to increase her celebrity, and by the time her fake marriage was annulled, she'd have everything she ever dreamed of.

Just as Harper said.

Chapter 8

What have I gotten myself into? Azure wondered for the second time that day. The first time she had the thought was when she was at the Fountain, checking out their private dining rooms with Harper. He'd been attentive and affectionate the entire appointment. A touch on her shoulder, a kiss on her check, a hand on her waist while they selected the flowers and table linens. By the time they parted ways, Azure was so hot, so overcome with desire, she had to drink a glass of cold water to cool down. But three hours later, her body was still throbbing with need.

Armed with the dozens of wedding dress photos she'd downloaded onto her cell phone, and Harper's suggestions at the front of her mind, she'd left the Fountain that afternoon bound and determined to find the gown of her dreams. Only, after hours of shopping in trendy, upscale boutiques, she hadn't tried on a single dress that wowed her.

"What about this one?" The salesgirl, a bubbly strawberry-blonde who'd fit in perfectly with the cast of *Glee,* held up a ruffled, multicolored minidress. "You said you were looking for something fun, and this sexy number screams 'I came to party!'"

"I'm looking for something a little less Katy Perry and a lot more Audrey Hepburn," Azure explained, wearing a soft smile. A Philadelphia landmark synonymous with high living, Mystique was often frequented by the rich and famous, and as Azure glanced around the women's section she spotted several local celebrities. The mayor's wife, a sitcom star and a news anchor were all enjoying a complimentary glass of champagne in the adjoining hair salon.

"Don't worry. We'll find the right dress. I'm sure of it."

I wish I shared your confidence, Azure thought, feeling her hope wane. Mystique carried the largest selection of formal attire in the city, and Azure knew if she couldn't find a dress here, she wouldn't find it anywhere. Dresses, shoes and accessories were positioned on eye-catching end displays. The scent of lavender was heavy in the air, and brides in poufy designer dresses sashayed around the store like a fashion show. "Do you carry Vanessa Hamilton's line?"

"Of course!" the clerk replied cheerfully. "She is *the* designer to watch this season, and a Philly native, as well."

"Yes, I know. I'm a huge fan of her work."

"Her collection is to die for, but it's also rather steep. I don't remember if I asked you earlier, but is there a price point you're comfortable being at?"

"I haven't given it much thought. The right dress is invaluable, and I really want to look special tomorrow night."

Dollar signs glistened in the consultant's eyes. "What's the occasion?"

"A dinner party." Azure felt silly for lying, but she'd promised Harper she wouldn't tell anyone about their surprise wedding ceremony, and she was going to honor her word.

"I want a dress that will knock my fiancé's socks off, but it has to be tasteful, classy, the type of gown that makes a bold statement."

Azure cringed when she heard the excitement in her voice, the sheer, unadulterated joy. The word *fiancé* felt funny on her lips, and as foreign to her ears as bluegrass music. A month ago, she'd been lusting after Harper Hamilton from afar, but in less than twenty-four hours she would be his lawfully wedded wife. Sure, in name only, but playing house with Harper for the next three months was a hell of a lot better than sitting on her couch watching reality TV night after night.

Patting back a yawn, Azure rolled her stiff, aching shoulders to loosen the knots in her back. Nervous excitement prevented her from getting a good night's sleep. That *and* the raunchy, X-rated dream she'd had about Harper. It was the second one she'd had that week, and it was only Tuesday! *Only God knows how I'm going to survive living with him,* she thought, as her favorite parts of last night's dream flashed in her mind. *It's only a matter of time before I do something stupid like—*

Shrieks and applause pierced the air. Startled by the noise, Azure glanced over her shoulder. A brunette in a lace A-line gown was standing in front of a mirror, fanning a hand to her tear-streaked face, and an older woman was sobbing into a lace-trimmed handkerchief. *Has to be her mother,* Azure thought, watching the touching scene unfold. Soon, everyone was crying, including their stoic-faced consultant with the bouffant hairstyle.

Azure felt a pang of guilt and wondered how her mom and sister would feel if they knew she was shopping for a wedding dress without them. They were too busy, too wrapped up in their own lives, and probably wouldn't care. That suited Azure fine. Truth be told, she didn't want her fault-finding mother or sister around. They'd just point out her flaws and imperfections, anyway. Better she go at it alone, like the Lone Ranger.

But as Azure turned away to resume her search for the perfect gown, she felt her eyes moisten and her mouth dry. Suddenly, being in the boutique, surrounded by glowing brides and their weeping mothers, made Azure feel sad, insignificant, as though she didn't matter. *What else is new?* she thought, swallowing hard. *I've felt that way since the day Eden was born.*

"This dress would look amazing on you!"

Azure blinked, swung her gaze back around to her cheerful, rosy-cheeked consultant.

"What do you think?" she asked, holding an ivory gown with a plunging neckline out in front of her. "Zoe Saldana wore this Vanessa Hamilton number to a movie premiere back in July, and fashionistas are *still* raving about it!"

The slinky satin gown looked more like a nightgown than a wedding dress, and the only thing Azure liked about it was the color. "No, thanks. It's not my style."

"But this dress was made for a woman like you. Someone tall, with toned arms and gorgeous, mile-long legs."

A sheepish smile tickled Azure's lips. She didn't know if the clerk was telling the truth or buttering her up to make a sale, but she agreed to try on the dress and after selecting several more gowns from Vanessa Hamilton's collection, she followed her consultant into the fitting room area. The first dress she squeezed into felt tighter than plastic wrap, the second one was five inches too short and the bejeweled halter made her look like a human Pop-Tart.

Hands on her hips, her face pinched with frustration, Azure carefully studied herself in the three-way mirror. Hating how dumpy she looked in the strapless gown, she sucked in a breath. *Maybe Mom's right. Maybe I should lose some weight.*

Azure was ready to throw in the towel, to call it a day, but at the last minute, she decided to try on the ivory gown the salesgirl had brought out. From the moment Azure stepped into the formfitting satin, she knew it was the dress she was going to marry Harper in. It had a deep side split, fit her body like a second skin and accentuated all of her best assets.

Azure spun to the left and to the right. Silencing her inner critic—who sounded a lot like her mom—she slipped a hand down her stomach and hips. Azure loved how the material kissed her curves, loved how it made her look long and lean. According to Harper, she had a great figure. He'd said so last night while they were having dinner, and that morning when Azure was chastising herself for eating too many free hors d'oeuvres at the Fountain. At the thought of Harper, goose bumps pricked her skin. This time tomorrow, she'd be Mrs. Harper Hamilton. It was a heady thought, one that brought on a fresh wave of butterflies.

Someone knocked on the door.

"Is everything okay in there?"

Azure nodded, though her consultant couldn't see her. "Yes, thanks, I'm fine."

"Do you need help with the zipper?"

"No, I'm good."

A pause, then, "If you need anything just holler. I'm right outside the fitting room."

Twirling around, a wide smile on her face, she marveled at how glamorous she looked in the expensive Vanessa Hamilton gown. *God, I hope Harper likes this dress.*

Azure cast her eyes over her shoulder and stared at her backside in the mirror. Her butt looked huge, but that was no surprise. The dress was satin, ivory and clung to every curve and slope. And it was perfect. Exactly what she was looking for.

Back in the boutique, Azure perused the shoe section, in

search of a pair of killer pumps to complement her backless gown. "Oh wow, these are hot!" she gushed, grabbing the silver, open-toe pumps from off the display and sliding her foot inside. They were just what she was looking for. But at the wrong price.

Azure quickly decided the shoes were worth it. She had to get them. And if she raised the hem of her dress and dyed the heels ivory, she'd have the look she envisioned in her head. A chic, sophisticated ensemble she felt not only ridiculously sexy in but graceful, as well. The way Mrs. Harper Hamilton should.

Floating through the boutique, clutching her dream gown and shoes in her hands, Azure prayed she had enough money in her account to cover her purchases. Holding her breath, she watched as the salesclerk rang up each item, and when the total came up on the screen, Azure felt her body go numb. *Two thousand, five hundred and twenty-nine dollars!*

Azure opened her mouth to ask the thin, middle-aged clerk to cancel the transaction, then remembered Harper had given her an envelope when they were chatting outside the Fountain. "If it's not enough, then just send me a text with your bank info and I'll deposit more money into your account," he'd said as they parted ways.

Rooting around in her purse, she searched frantically for the envelope. When she found it buried underneath her makeup case, she ripped it open. Azure gasped so loud the salesclerk flinched. Azure shook her head, unable to believe what her eyes were seeing. The envelope was filled with dozens of crisp, one-hundred dollar bills. *All this money for a dress and a pair of shoes?* After she paid for her outfit, she'd have enough left over to get her makeup, hair and nails professionally done for tomorrow night, and it was all thanks to Harper.

Ten minutes later, Azure sailed out of the boutique, shopping bags in hand and pep in her step. The clear night sky was a vivid array of deep, breathtaking blues and the air held a sweet, pomaceous aroma that made Azure hanker for a slice of apple pie. As she strode down the street, she made up her mind not to let anything ruin her day. Not her looming deadline, her self-doubts or the gridlocked traffic that stretched as far back as the expressway.

Hearing her ring tone, Azure stopped at a taxi stand and pulled her cell phone out of her purse. "Hello?"

"Hi, Azure. It's me, Harper."

Hearing Harper's voice made Azure feel light on her feet, made her insides turn to mush every time. To hear him above the noise on the traffic-congested road, she plugged her ear and turned away from the busy street.

"How did things go this afternoon? Did you find what you were looking for?"

"Yes, thanks to you."

"I'm just glad the money was enough."

"I bought the perfect dress!" Azure gushed, unable to contain her excitement. "It's long, and fitted, and makes me look ten pounds thinner!"

"I bet it looks incredible on you. Everything does."

A girly smile exploded across her face.

"I'm just calling to make sure tomorrow night is still a go."

"Why, are you having second thoughts?"

"About marrying you? Never."

Beaming brighter than a beacon, she sighed and rested a hand on her chest. Azure had never met a man who was so inherently sweet. Just imagining the scene in her mind—she and Harper gazing at each other as they exchanged vows in front of his family and their friends—made her feel downright giddy. Playing Harper's wife was going to be fun, the chance of a lifetime, and Azure planned to use her fifteen minutes of fame to boost her career. *It's time I quit cover-*

ing news stories and be *a news story,* she decided. *That's the only way I'm going to keep my job* and *make my mom proud.*

"I picked up the marriage license this afternoon and confirmed the time and location with the officiant," Harper explained. "I'll pick you up at your condo at five o'clock sharp—"

"We're going to the Fountain together?"

"Yes, why, is that a problem?"

Azure grew so flushed she couldn't string together a coherent sentence. "Well, um, no…it's just that it's bad luck for the groom to see the bride before the wedding," she blurted out.

"You're right, it is. I forgot."

"It's not a big deal. Forget I said anything."

"I'll have a town car pick you up instead."

"No, Harper, I don't want to put you out."

"You're not," he assured her.

"Are you sure?"

"Positive. I want everything to be perfect, and it will be. Trust me."

Azure heard the smile in his voice, heard how relaxed he sounded. "Oh," she said, struck by a thought, "don't forget to bring the prenup tomorrow. I can sign it before the ceremony, and the minister can witness it for us."

"A prenup?" Harper repeated, his voice filled with surprise. "We don't need one. When you get an annulment, neither spouse is entitled to any money or compensation once the union is dissolved."

"I know, but I'd feel better if we had one. I don't want people to call me a gold digger, and if I don't sign a prenup, those catty bloggers from Black, Rich and Fly will crucify me!"

"Are you sure about this?"

"Positive. Draft the agreement and bring it with you to tomorrow night."

"Yes, ma'am. I'm on it!"

His tone lightened the mood, relieved the tension Azure was feeling inside. All day she'd been wrestling with her conscience, weighing the pros and cons of marrying for publicity, but speaking to Harper had a calming effect on her. "This is probably the last time we'll speak before tomorrow night, huh?"

"If anything changes just give me a ring on my cell phone."

Azure nodded, promised she would. "Sleep well."

"Good night. I'll see you at the altar."

Azure disconnected the call. Feeling lighthearted and free, she dropped her cell phone in her purse, scooped up her purchases and strode confidently down Madison Avenue. She smiled at the couples strolling hand in hand, the families lined up outside the movie theater and the homeless man dancing to the music streaming out of the Irish pub. Azure felt like doing a little jig of her own. Imagine, she—a former klutz who never had a single friend in high school—was marrying a Hamilton!

Azure couldn't wait to tell her mother the news. She'd probably faint. And not just because she was on a strict five-hundred-calorie diet, either. Her mother would be stunned, so tongue-tied she wouldn't be able to speak. And for some strange reason that thought caused a big, fat smile to cover Azure's face. One that she couldn't wipe away no matter how hard she tried.

Chapter 9

"Azure, it's time." Harper waited, listened for a moment, then knocked on the washroom door. Standing in the private staff wing of the Fountain five minutes before the wedding was supposed to start was making Harper nervous. And it wasn't on the schedule he'd drawn up last night, either. He should be downstairs, in the banquet hall, going over the ceremony with the officiant, not searching for his runaway bride. "Hello? Azure? Are you in there?"

Nothing.

Harper scratched his head. Had she come out of the ladies' room without him noticing her? He'd been on his phone, reading all the frantic texts from his parents and brothers, and had lost track of time. His family was downstairs, seated in the banquet hall, probably wondering what the hell was going on. By now, they'd seen the elaborate flower displays, the rose-scattered aisle and the chocolate cupcake tower. No doubt they'd put two and two together and figured out he'd in-

vited them to his surprise wedding and not a family business meeting. And now it was showtime. Everyone was there. Everything was in place. All he had to do now was find Azure.

"I can't do this."

At the sound of Azure's voice coming from the ladies' room, Harper released the breath he'd been holding. He clasped his hands together and stared up at the ceiling. *Thank you, God.* All wasn't lost. He could still pull off the biggest publicity stunt of the year. And score more press than a tween pop superstar slapped with a paternity suit.

"I know I agreed to marry you, but I can't. I'm so scared I'm shaking like a leaf."

Harper tried the lock, jiggled it. "Azure, let me in."

"No."

"Why not?"

"Because it's bad luck—"

"For the groom to see the bride before the ceremony," he finished with a slow nod. Harper wanted to remind Azure that their wedding was just a publicity stunt, an over-the-top event to garner free press, but he didn't say any of those things. He had to talk her off the ledge and into the banquet hall where their guests were impatiently waiting, and reminding her of the terms of their deal wouldn't help any.

Clearing his throat, he braced his hands against the oak door. It was time to employ the Hamilton charm, and not a moment too soon. He'd worked too hard and invested too much time and energy into his plan to sit back and watch it fall apart now. "It's normal to be scared, Azure. Every bride's nervous on her wedding day, even celebrities. I read somewhere that Reese Witherspoon chipped a tooth on her wedding day, and apparently Beyoncé threw up twice before she married Jay-Z."

"You're lying," she accused, the anxiety in her voice giving way to amusement. "I'm the biggest Beyoncé fan ever, and if she'd puked on her wedding day, I would have known about it!"

"You can do this, Azure. I know you can. Just think of tonight as one big party, and when we finish cutting the cake and posing for pictures, we'll go next door and crash in our suite."

"Our suite?"

"Yeah, I got us a room at the St. Regis Hotel."

Her tone grew softer, serious. "You did?"

"Of course. And not just any room. The honeymoon suite."

"Get out!"

Harper chuckled. Again. He did a lot of that when Azure was around. "What kind of husband would I be if I didn't get my wife the best suite in town?" he asked, hoping he was softening her up and alleviating her fears. "Azure, please come out. I need you. You're the only person I want to play my wife, and if you bail on me now, I'll look like a fool again."

A moment of silence passed.

"Okay, Harper, you win. I think I'm ready to do this."

"Great. We'll walk into the banquet hall together, and—"

"No way," Azure quipped, her tone filled with fire and sass. "This is my moment to shine, and no offense, but I'm not sharing the spotlight with you!"

Spoken like a true woman, he thought, indulging in a grin. One minute, Azure was refusing to come out of the ladies' room, and the next she was calling the shots. Harper liked that. Liked being with someone who wasn't afraid to stand up to him or speak her mind.

"Harper, did you remember to bring the prenup?"

"Yes, the officiant has it. But like I said earlier, we really don't need one."

"I know, I know," she singsonged. "Just humor me, okay, Mr. Hot Shot Attorney?"

Harper chuckled. Azure never failed to make him laugh,

to make him feel like a kid again. That's why she was the perfect person to play his wife. There was never a dull moment when she was around, and he'd cracked up more in the last week than he had the whole month. "Oh, and one last thing..."

"Yes?"

"Smile for the cameras."

"I smile all the time."

"Not enough," he countered, "and that's a shame because your smile is truly a thing of beauty. It lights your eyes, warms your face and brightens every room you enter."

"Harper, stop. You're making me even *more* nervous."

"I'm telling the truth, Azure. I could never, ever get enough of your smile. It's as stunning as a dozen sunsets, and the single most beautiful thing I've ever seen."

Azure giggled. "You shouldn't be practicing law, you should be writing for Hallmark!"

"I can't wait to see you strutting down the aisle," he confessed, once her laughter died down. "I'm leaving now, Azure, but I'll meet you at the altar in ten minutes. I'll be the guy in the charcoal-gray tuxedo, standing beside the officiant, who only has eyes for you."

She'll show, she'll show, he told himself, turning around and striding down the hallway. Harper thought about his ex, thought about all the times she'd disappointed him over the course of their relationship, and wondered if Azure was capable of hurting him, too. He shook off his doubts, ignored the heavy feeling in his heart. Azure wasn't his ex. Sure, he didn't know her that well, and they'd only hatched their plan a week or so ago, but his gut was telling him Azure was someone he could trust.

Your gut, huh? jeered his inner voice. *The last time you listened to your gut you ended up dating a woman who cheated on you with a chubby, gold-toothed rapper!*

Harper stopped outside the banquet hall, took a minute to

catch his breath and clear his mind. He felt confident, strong and loved how his sleek tux made him look powerful, like the man in charge. This was the moment he'd been waiting for, the day he thought would never come. Stealing the spotlight from his cousin Jake was sure to boost his celebrity, and after today, everyone would know his name. But as Harper straightened his tie, he wasn't thinking about the media buzz his surprise nuptials were sure to generate. His thoughts were on Azure. On the saucy, sassy sister he couldn't seem to get out of his mind. He was going to enjoy being her husband. For the next three months, he had the pleasure of seeing the titillating magazine writer every morning and every night.

Harper strode through the banquet hall doors, and into the quaint private room, feeling like that man. Azure Ellison's man. At the thought, a broad grin eclipsed his face.

Six long strides, and Harper was at the altar, standing beside the silver-haired officiant with the jovial Father Christmas disposition. Seconds ticked by on the wall clock Harper fixed his gaze on. He stood straight, with his hands clasped in front of him, trying to ignore the quizzical looks on the faces of his parents. The tension in the room was high, as if everyone was holding their collective breath. The whole family was there except for Nelson. His brother had landed a small role in the new Spike Lee movie and wouldn't be back in town until the charity banquet his aunt Jeanette was hosting next month.

Out of the corner of his eye, he saw his family members exchanging worried glances. Guilt troubled his conscience, made his stomach feel queasy. Deceiving the people he loved went against everything Harper stood for, but to compete with his cousin Jake he had to fight fire with fire, and his plan was sure to boost his popularity.

Searching the crowd, he found his cousin Jake and his fiancée, Charlotte, seated at the round table closest to the stage.

Jake was fidgeting with his cuff links, moving around in his satin-draped seat. Harper swallowed a laugh. His cousin was jealous, so wound up that Harper could almost see the steam shooting out of his ears. *Perfect,* he thought, *my plan is already working.*

The male pianist began playing the Wedding March, and a hush fell over the crowd. Harper stared at the banquet room doors. Anxious to see his bride, he peered down the rose-scattered aisle, hoping to be the first one to catch a glimpse of her. This was the moment of truth. Was Azure going to join him at the altar, or had she already bolted out the back door?

Harper tried to clear his mind of all doubts, of all misgivings. But his fears persisted. Standing on the podium, in front of his family and friends, waiting for Azure to appear was stressful, as nerve-racking as testifying in front of the grand jury. The truth was, Harper was looking forward to playing house with Azure. To getting to know her better, to discovering her likes and dislikes, to seeing her in those itty-bitty workout shorts again. But when the clock struck six, and she didn't appear at the banquet hall doors as planned, his hope faded. His disappointment was so heavy, so crushing, it felt as if a bowling ball had been dropped on his chest. And it hurt like hell.

The silver-haired officiant cleared his throat, then leaned over and whispered, "Maybe you should go check on her again. Your bride-to-be probably has a terrible case of the jitters and…" His eyes spread wide. "My, oh, my…"

Whispers and gasps pierced the air. Harper swung back around, and when he saw Azure standing expectantly in the doorway of the banquet hall, a vision in ivory satin and blinding sapphire diamonds, his jaw hit his chest with a painful thud.

Their eyes met, collided with the force of two high-speed, out-of-control freight trains.

Harper followed Azure with his eyes, through the doors, past the twenty-foot chocolate waterfall, down the straight, narrow aisle. Her face, like her hair and skin, had a natural, healthy glow. Azure glided into the hall with inherent grace, moved in slow, gliding steps that commanded the attention of every bewildered-looking guest.

Azure was trembling, so scared out of her mind, she pictured herself fleeing through the emergency doors. It took all her effort to breathe and walk at the same time. All eyes were on her, and the realization made her stomach coil into a dozen knots. She wasn't used to being the center of attention. That was Eden's gig. Not hers. She was the smart, educated one, not the sexy, titillating one who craved male attention.

Wrestling with her conscience about her surprise wedding increased her anxiety. Azure's nerves were wrought, and her legs felt heavy, as if they were coated in cold, wet clay. Her personal demons, rooted in her childhood, were tormenting her, and all Azure could hear in her mind were the cruel taunts of her peers. And her mother. She'd always felt that she wasn't good enough, that she didn't belong, and her family reinforced that belief on a daily basis.

No one's ever going to marry you looking like that.... Sis, if you were more disciplined like me, you would have a slim, gorgeous body, too.... Of course your father and I love you. We just want you to look your best and represent the family well....f

To steady her nerves, she needed to focus on something, on someone with a warm demeanor, but Azure couldn't find a single friendly face in the crowd. And when her gaze landed on her boss, her eyes narrowed in confusion. Leland was holding a piece of Kleenex to his eyes, and his shoulders were convulsing violently. *Oh God, is he crying?* The thought made

a giggle rise in her throat. Leland got a kick out of bullying his employees, but deep down the man was a big old softie.

Azure concentrated on her breathing, ensured that her nerves didn't get the best of her. Lightbulbs flashed in her face, but she was too nervous to smile for the cameras. Her gaze locked in on Harper, and when their eyes met, Azure felt her heart bounce up into her throat. *Oh my,* she thought, gripping her bouquet. *He's gorgeous!* Harper was a sharp dresser who looked great in everything, but his sleek charcoal-gray tuxedo, crisp white dress shirt and polished black shoes gave him star power. Charm oozed from his pores, and his energy was so imposing, so powerful, her body hummed with desire.

"You are the most beautiful bride I have ever seen, Azure, and I feel so honored to be sharing this moment with you," Harper said, offering his right hand. When Azure laced her fingers through his, a bolt of electricity ripped through him. Harper felt himself go hard and hoped that none of their guests saw the giant bulge in his pants.

"Friends, family and well-wishers, I want to thank each and every one of you for coming tonight to witness the union of these two people…" the officiant began, sweeping his hands toward the guests seated at the round, satin-draped tables.

Harper didn't hear a word the officiant said. Not a single one. His gaze was fixed on Azure, and he didn't have the power to turn away. His thoughts took him down a rocky road. A road he had no business being on. He was hungry for her. So turned on by her floral scent, her slinky, fitted dress and her tight, lush curls he couldn't think of anything else but making love to her. All Harper cared about was seeing what she had on under her dress. The thought consumed him, made it impossible for him to focus on anything else.

Pressing his eyes shut, he struck the thought from his mind. He knew better than to touch her. Their marriage was for show, and if he ever crossed the line, Azure would never forgive him. And he didn't want to do anything to jeopardize their friendship.

"Harper, please repeat after me…"

Harper recited his vows, and as he promised to love, honor and cherish her all the days of his life, he saw Azure's eyes fill with tears. He lowered his voice, moved closer. Got so close he could see the tiny freckles on her nose. "Are you okay?" he whispered, his face pinched with concern. "Have you changed your mind about all this? Do you want me to stop?"

"Yes. No. Oh, I don't know."

Cupping her face in his hands, he smoothed his thumbs over the apples of her cheeks, then tenderly caressed her neck and shoulders. His touch had a profound effect on her. Her breathing slowed, her hands stopped shaking and her fears evaporated like water on a hot, sunny day. Harper spoke softly to her, and his praise bolstered her confidence. He said she was beautiful, that he'd never seen a more stunning bride, that he cared about her deeply. His words moved her, filled her with calm and peace. It was a sweet, magical moment, one Azure would cherish forever, for as long as she lived.

"I'm okay," Azure told the officiant. "Let's continue."

The officiant lifted a velvet ring box off the podium, opened it and nodded at Harper.

Harper took Azure's left hand, cradled it gently in his palm. Sliding the ring onto her fourth finger, he said in a clear, confident voice, "I, Harper James Hamilton, take you, Azure Ellison, to be my lawfully wedded wife, to have and to hold from this day forward, for better or for worse, for richer or poorer, in sickness and in health, till death do us part."

Azure blinked, stared down incredulously at the wedding ring Harper had just slid on her finger. The three-carat diamond was the size of a jawbreaker and flanked by dozens of delicate, pear-shaped stones. Azure's head was spinning a hundred miles an hour, and the more she stared at the enormous rock, the more convinced she was that this was all a wonderful dream.

The officiant gestured to the box, and Azure took out the platinum Cartier wedding band she'd selected for Harper while out shopping the day before.

Using her bouquet as a shield, Azure rested a hand on her stomach, hoping the act would quiet her fears. But the butterflies remained, fluttering and flittering around her belly in earnest. Harper rested a hand on the base of her neck and gave a light squeeze. The gesture calmed her, reminded her that they were in this together. Lifting her chin, Azure looked him straight in the eye and confidently recited her vows.

"Tonight, we have all witnessed the union of these two souls and the ultimate demonstration of their love. May they both remain faithful to their vows, committed to their marriage and steadfast in their growing love. I now pronounce Harper and Azure husband and wife," the officiant said in a loud booming voice. "And now for the moment Harper has been waiting for all night. Son, you may—"

Before the words left the officiant's mouth, Harper kissed her. He wrapped her up so tightly in his arms, Azure could feel his heart beating through his tuxedo jacket. The kiss was slow, thoughtful, but caused delicious shudders to pass through her. Her flesh burned with desire, her nipples strained against the soft, shimmery material of her dress and her hands grew clammy with sweat. Azure groaned something fierce, released an audible plea that would make an exotic dancer blush. Her bouquet slipped from her grasp and dropped to the floor with a thud. Azure decided to retrieve it later, *after* she was finished kissing her new husband.

Harper cupped her face, and Azure layered her hands over his. The kiss kindled her passion. Her pulse raced, accelerated into overdrive, and every nerve in her body tingled and shuddered. Lost in the sensual whirlwind of their embrace, she pressed her body flat against his and shamelessly kissed the man she'd lusted after since high school with everything she had. *I could never get enough of this,* she thought, tenderly stroking the back of Harper's head. *Never, ever, not for a million years.*

For a moment, Azure forgot that they were standing in the banquet hall, surrounded by their family and friends. But when the officiant loudly cleared his throat and pried them apart, Azure came crashing back down to reality.

Holding a microphone in his hand, the pianist stood and addressed the well-dressed guests. "Please join me in welcoming Mr. and Mrs. Harper Hamilton to the dance floor!"

The audience was dead quiet. No one moved, spoke or blinked an eye.

"Come on, Azure. It's time for our first dance as husband and wife."

"B-but we don't have a song."

Harper winked at her. "Of course we do."

Azure's smile masked her fear. Of course Harper had selected a song. Nothing got past him. He was the King of Cool, a debonair mastermind who never overlooked anything.

Harper took Azure's hand and led her toward the dimly lit dance floor. There was a smattering of applause, and as they crossed the room, Azure noticed all the stunned expressions on their guests' faces. The only people who seemed to be enjoying themselves were her teary, champagne-guzzling boss and Maggie. Her roommate was up on her feet, waving wildly and snapping pictures with her cell phone.

When Azure heard the opening bar of the song "This I Promise You"—the one she used to listen to religiously when she was in tenth grade—her heart melted to a puddle at her feet. The tender love ballad brought back memories of high school, of all the times she'd sat in the cafeteria watching Harper, or writing in her journal under her favorite oak tree.

How did Harper know this was her favorite love song of all time? Harper Hamilton was truly something. Not only was he charming, but he was by far the most romantic man she had ever met. And when Harper bent down and brushed his lips across hers, Azure prayed he'd be in her life forever.

"Azure…" he breathed, sliding his arms around her waist and caressing her hips. "This dress is something else."

"Do you think it's too much?"

"I think it's perfect. You couldn't look any more beautiful."

"I can't take any of the credit. Your mom is an incredible fashion designer."

"You're right, she is, but that dress was nothing but a piece of fabric until *you* put it on."

Cradling her in his arms, he murmured words of admiration and praise in her ear. Azure swayed to the music, moved slowly against Harper's tall, athletic body. Her breathing increased, came in quick, short gulps. Desire rose, grew to crushing heights. Azure didn't know if she could pretend to be Harper's wife for the next three months without crossing the line. Or rather diving over it. She wasn't a raging sex fiend, and she'd rather clean her house than sweat out her perm having sex, but every time Harper touched her, she wanted to ride him until she was spent.

And that's my tamest fantasy, she thought, ignoring the tingles pulsing between her legs. The song ended, and the emcee invited guests to join the happy couple on the dance floor. No one moved.

Azure didn't mind one bit. She liked being alone with Harper and enjoyed being in his arms so much she draped her arms casually around his neck as they moved and swayed together to the slow, sensual Whitney Houston number playing.

"Wow, the emcee went deep into the musical vault for this one," Harper joked.

"When I was a little girl I wanted to be Whitney Houston so bad."

"You did? Why?"

"Because I thought if I was thin and pretty my life would be perfect."

"Azure, baby, you are all those things and more."

"Not according to my mom." The words slipped out of her mouth before she could stop them.

"Then when I meet Mrs. Ellison I'm going to have some very harsh words for her."

"You do not know my mom."

"But I know you," he said softly, drawing his finger along her cheek, "and you're a smart, captivating woman, a woman any man in this room would kill to have on his arm."

Azure felt her eyes began to itch and burn, but she checked herself before she lost her cool. Harper was acting, saying and doing all the right things, gazing longingly at her, pretending he was a groom who was madly in love. The attorney was giving their friends and family one hell of a show. It was all for publicity's sake, a scheme he'd cooked up one night at the bar after too many drinks, and she'd be a fool to forget it.

If this is all for show, she wondered, resting her head on Harper's chest and closing her eyes, *then why does it feel like the real thing?*

Chapter 10

"Congratulations, roomie! I'm so happy for you!" Maggie shrieked, rushing over to the dessert table and throwing her thick, fleshy arms around Azure's neck.

Giggling, Azure hugged her roommate back. "You really mean that, Maggie?"

"Of course I do! Why wouldn't I be happy for you? You're one of my closest friends."

"I know, but I thought you'd come down on me for marrying Harper. You said, and I quote, 'Only a truly desperate woman would marry a man she just met.'"

"Oh, I still think you're crazy for trying the knot, but who am I to judge?" she said with a shrug. "But now that you're moving in with Harper, you can sublet your room to Greg, so I don't have to travel halfway across town to see him. See, roomie, everybody wins!"

"You just couldn't wait to get rid of me," Azure teased,

wearing a sad face. "Some friend you are. I haven't even packed my stuff, but you're already showing me the door."

"Damn right! And I can't wait to be an auntie, so hurry up and get knocked up!"

The women laughed. Perusing the dessert table, arm in arm, they sampled each sweet, gooey dessert and discussed their new living arrangements. Laughing and joking with Maggie helped Azure to relax, and she was having such a good time chatting with her roommate she didn't notice Harper's mother standing behind her until Maggie acknowledged her presence with a friendly wave. Mrs. Hamilton did not return the gesture.

Maggie plopped a handful of chocolate éclairs onto her plate, grabbed a bottle of wine and rushed off. Azure had never seen her friend move so fast, but when she saw Mrs. Hamilton's pursed lips and narrowed eyes, she understood why her roommate ran for cover. Fear drenched Azure's skin, and her heartbeat drummed painfully in her ears.

"I have to admit, Ms. Ellison, you do look amazing in that dress."

Licking the dryness from her lips, Azure nodded and clasped her hands out in front of her. "Thank you, Mrs. Hamilton. That means a lot coming from you. And congratulations on the success of your new fall line. It's received rave reviews, and last week Sarah Jessica Parker tweeted that your fashion show at the Metropolitan Pavilion was outstanding."

"I had no idea Sarah tweeted about the event," she said, her tone losing its cold, hard edge. "Maybe that's why my phone has been ringing off the hook."

"I'm not surprised. I love fashion, and wear all of the top designers, but your line is by far my favorite this season."

Mrs. Hamilton raised a thin, perfectly sculptured eyebrow. "It is?"

"By far. I love that your pieces are timeless and elegant

and ultrafeminine." Staring down at her dress, she touched a hand to the embellished neckline and indulged in a dreamy smile. "I feel so glamorous in this gown, and Harper keeps telling me how beautiful I look."

Mrs. Hamilton's eyes caught fire.

Azure searched her mind for something to say, something that would put Mrs. Hamilton back in a good mood. "I'm sorry you weren't able to attend last month's photo shoot—"

"I'm not," she said tightly, crossing her arms. "I didn't come over here to shoot the breeze with you, Ms. Ellison, or to hear how great you think my family is. I came over here to discuss your relationship with my son."

Azure gulped.

"You're an attractive woman, and from what I've heard a fine writer, but that doesn't mean I think you're the right woman for my son. I don't."

Sensing a threat, Azure searched the room for Harper. Guests were mingling around the banquet hall, posing for pictures and admiring the chocolate cupcake tower, but her tall, dark and handsome groom was nowhere to be found.

"You're not the kind of person Harper needs in his life."

To that, Azure had nothing to say. She refused to get into an argument with Mrs. Hamilton, or admit that their wedding was a publicity stunt, so she remained quiet.

"I don't know much about you, Mrs. Ellison, but I know I don't like you." Her face was ageless, free of blemishes and imperfections, but when she scowled, wrinkles creased her forehead. "You remind me of Harper's ex-fiancée. She was a sly, opportunistic—"

"Ex-fiancée!" Azure stumbled over the word. "Harper said they weren't serious."

"He lied to you. My son loved that girl with all his heart." Mrs. Hamilton sniffed, blinked back the tears that had filled her eyes. "She broke his heart. I'm his mother. I should know."

"That's terrible.... I had no idea, Mrs. Hamilton. Harper never told me."

Mrs. Hamilton spoke through clenched teeth, and when she shook her head, her diamond teardrop earrings swung furiously back and forth. "I'm not going to stand by idly and let you or anyone else play my son for a fool again."

"I would never do anything to hurt Harper."

"That's what his ex said. Then the hussy cheated on him with some fat, tattooed rapper!"

Azure stepped back and bumped into the dessert table.

"Maybe you can help me figure out what's going on, because frankly this shotgun wedding doesn't make any sense. Harper is a meticulous planner, who doesn't act impulsively or do anything by happenstance, so there must be a very compelling reason why he married you."

"You're right, Mrs. Hamilton. There is." Azure paused for effect and to steady her frazzled nerves, but when she opened her mouth to speak, Mrs. Hamilton cut her off.

"I have a feeling there's a lot more to your whirlwind romance than meets the eye, Ms. Ellison. I don't understand the rush to get married. From what I gather, you've only been dating my son for a few short weeks."

"We're so madly and desperately in love we..." Azure paused, tried to recall what she'd heard on *The Bachelorette* during last season's finale. "...that we can't stand to be apart from each other, and we wanted to make things official as soon as possible."

Mrs. Hamilton lowered her gaze to Azure's stomach. "Is there maybe something *else* you recently discovered that you'd care to share, Ms. Ellison?"

Azure boldly met Mrs. Hamilton's glare. The question was carefully worded, but Azure was skilled at reading between the lines and knew exactly what Harper's mother was getting at. "I'm not pregnant," Azure replied, keeping her tone even and her temper in check. "And I didn't pressure Harper to marry me, either. He popped the question, and I said yes."

"You liar!"

Mrs. Hamilton's outburst caught the attention of the guests chatting at the bar. Azure swallowed the lump in her throat. Her body was on fire, a sweltering two hundred degrees and rising fast. This showdown with Mrs. Hamilton ranked right up there with the day her mom announced—in front of all their family and friends—that Azure would be attending fat camp in Arizona. *Oh great,* Azure thought miserably, wiping the perspiration dotting her hairline, *my boss heard every word and is salivating like a dog with a steak bone.*

"I don't know what game you're playing, Ms. Ellison, or what you're after, but you're never going to see a dime of my family's money."

"Harper and I signed a prenup—"

"Of course you did," she spat, clutching her pearl necklace in her hands. "Harper's an attorney. He wouldn't marry you without one. I don't care how pretty you are."

"No, actually I suggested it."

Surprise clouded Mrs. Hamilton's oval brown face.

"Harper said we didn't need one, but I insisted."

Her opponent's lips parted, but no words came out.

"I knew people would think that I only married Harper for his money, and I didn't want to give the haters a leg to stand on."

Mrs. Hamilton looked deflated, defeated, but quickly recovered. "Just know this," she began, the hard edge back in her voice, "if you hurt my son or humiliate him or this family in any way, you'll have to answer to me."

"With all due respect, Mrs. Hamilton, you don't know me or what I stand for."

"You're right, I don't, but I know your type. All you care about is advancing your career, and once you get what you're after, you'll be on to the next man. Probably a fat, tattooed rapper just like the last floozy my son dated!"

Did she just call me a floozy? Azure opened her mouth to give Mrs. Hamilton a piece of her mind—a piece that was fueled by rage—but when she felt a strong arm slide around her waist, she swallowed the blistering retort. Harper to the rescue, just in the nick of time. Taking in some air, Azure allowed his light, refreshing cologne to soothe her troubled mind and dissolve her murderous thoughts.

"There's my lovely bride." Harper hugged her to his chest and dropped a kiss on her cheek. "I've been looking all over for you, cupcake. Are you ready to cut the—"

"What an odd pet name. Wherever did it come from?" Mrs. Hamilton asked.

"When we were in high school, Azure baked me a batch of red velvet cupcakes, and they were so scrumptious I've been calling her Cupcake ever since."

It took everything in Azure's power not to crack up. *Me? Bake? Ha! I can't even make cookies in my goddaughter's Easy Bake Oven without burning them to a crisp!*

Mrs. Hamilton frowned. "You've known each other since high school?"

Harper's gaze darted between the two women. "Yes, of course, I thought Azure would have mentioned it. What exactly have you ladies been over here discussing all this time?"

"I was, um, just welcoming Azure to the family, Harper."

That was a welcome? A shiver tore down Azure's spine when she recalled the vicious threat Mrs. Hamilton had made, but when Harper glanced at her, she fervently nodded.

"I'd like to meet Azure's parents. Are they here?"

"Mr. and Mrs. Ellison really wish they could be here, Mom, but they're traveling out of the country and couldn't get back to the States on such short notice."

Harper wore a sad face, one that caused a giggle to tickle

Azure's throat. *Harper could give Pitt, Damon and Clooney a run for their money,* she thought, casting an admiring glance at her new husband. He was one hell of an actor and had convinced everyone—from his wary father to his shell-shocked brothers—that he was completely smitten with her.

"It looks like congratulations are in order!"

Azure watched Jake and his fiancée, Charlotte, approach, and smiled at the cozy twosome. They were standing arm in arm, so close it looked as if their bodies were fused together and were gazing longingly at each other. Azure thought they made a striking couple, who were sure to produce adorable kids, and wondered when they were going to tie the knot.

"This is the mother of all surprises, man." Chuckling, Jake clapped Harper on the back.

Mrs. Hamilton excused herself, and Azure finally released the breath she'd been holding. She'd never been so relieved to see someone leave, and when Mrs. Hamilton stomped back to her seat, Azure cheered inwardly. *Yes, there is a God!*

"We're glad that you and Charlotte could be here to share this wonderful occasion with us," Harper said, returning his arm to Azure's waist. "Right, Cupcake?"

Azure agreed. "It's great seeing you guys, and hopefully one day soon we can all get together for drinks or something. This time, I promise to leave my tape recorder at home!"

Everyone laughed.

"I have to admit," Jake conceded, his eyebrows raised and his head tilted in a questioning slant, "I didn't see this impromptu wedding ceremony coming!"

Harper shrugged. "It happens like that sometimes. I didn't see your engagement to Charlotte coming, either, and we all work together!"

"Yeah, but you knew I've been feeling Charlotte for a while."

"Yes, but I've been feeling Azure for *years*." Harper lowered his mouth to her face, stared intently at her. "From the moment I laid eyes on you in the halls of Willingham Prep, I knew you were the only girl for me. And from this day forward, I plan to treat you like the queen that you are. I'm going to make all your dreams come true. Every last one."

Azure knew she was wearing a dreamy expression on her face, but she couldn't stop her heart from going soft. She would never forget this moment—this magical, enchanted night—for as long as she lived. She was wearing a couture gown, thousands of dollars' worth of jewelry and a diamond wedding ring that was going to make her the envy of all her single friends. And best of all, Harper had kissed her! And it wasn't an innocent peck, either. He'd kissed her deeply, passionately, like a man hopelessly and desperately in love.

"We better let you two lovebirds cut the cake," Charlotte said, gesturing to the heavyset videographer who was filming them, "before things go from PG to too hot for TV!"

Still holding Azure to his side, Harper led her across the room to the round, glass table displaying their lavish cupcake tower. Guests gathered around, cameras poised, anxious to capture the moment. The mood in the banquet hall had changed from tense to festive, and their friends and family were teasing and laughing. Everyone was having a good time, but when Azure caught Mrs. Hamilton glaring at her, her smile fizzled. Harper's mother stood at the back of the room, her lips pursed into a furious scowl, and her hands clenched rigidly at her sides. Murder was in the fashion designer's eyes, and Azure knew she was the unlucky target.

Azure picked up the knife, clutched it so tightly her hands throbbed. *Now if Harper's mother attacks me I can defend myself.* The thought of her and Mrs. Hamilton duking it out in their designer gowns was so absurd Azure burst out laughing.

Harper frowned. "What's so funny?"

To stifle her giggles, she cleared the image from her mind

and gave her head a hard shake. "I was just thinking about that story you told your mom. You know, about me baking you cupcakes when we were in high school."

"I wasn't going for funny," he confessed. "I was going for sweet and endearing."

"That you are. And gorgeous, too."

Azure didn't realize the words had left her mouth until Harper leaned in, brushed his lips against her cheek and said loud enough for everyone in the room to hear, "You better stop flirting with me, Mrs. Hamilton, before I devour you like one of these here cupcakes!"

Feigning shock, Azure made her eyes big and wide, but inside she was praying earnestly that her new husband would make good on his threat.

Chapter 11

The honeymoon suite at the St. Regis Hotel was a magical, enchanted space, one filled with so many romantic touches Azure felt like Cinderella when she entered the spacious living room. Bronze pendant lamps showered the room with a soft, golden light, the exotic fruit in the heart-shaped gift basket sweetened the air, and the windows offered a panoramic view of downtown Philadelphia. The stars stretching the length of the deep blue sky hovered over the city like an umbrella, and from the twenty-fifth floor, the sight was nothing short of majestic.

"This place is incredible," Azure gushed, stunned by the view and the sultry ambience of the lavish suite. "I've stayed in a lot of great hotels, but nothing like this."

"If you think this is nice wait until you see the Sea of Cortez Resort in Cabo San Lucas. I don't impress easily, but their Oasis Suite blew me away."

"The closest I'll ever get to Mexico is Fiesta Night at Los Taquitos Restaurant!"

"We're going to have to do something about that, then." His smile was soft, filled with warmth and matched his light, easygoing tone. He was standing beside the mahogany desk, a mere breath away, and his cologne wafted toward her like a refreshing breeze. "I want us to go to Cabo San Lucas for Christmas and spend a few days at the Sea of Cortez Resort. It's always packed with celebrities, and we're bound to get some good press if we're there for all the holiday festivities."

"Harper, I can't afford a trip to Cabo."

"It won't cost you a thing," he said, assuring her. "And who knows, maybe you can score an interview with Diddy or Mariah, because they're always at the resort!"

Azure laughed, then promised to give it some more thought.

"You'll have a good time. I guarantee it."

There was a hitch in his tone, a catch that made her eyes zero in on his. The air was charged with tension, so thick and heavy it was difficult for Azure to breathe. Finally, after hours of mingling with their guests and posing for the cameras, they were alone. Completely alone. There were no waiters around offering champagne, no family members quizzing them about their dating history and Harper's mother wasn't shooting her dirty looks from across the room. It was their wedding night, and although the ceremony had been just for show, Azure couldn't help feeling let down. There'd be no kisses, no passionate embraces, no heartfelt words while making love and the thought of going to bed—alone—was depressing.

Tearing her gaze away from Harper's face, she stared outside the balcony window and out into the night sky. Azure hugged her arms to her chest. She needed a moment to think, to reflect on everything that had happened tonight. They'd pulled it off, the mother of all publicity stunts, but Azure felt more nervous now than when she was walking down the aisle.

"I almost forgot. This is for you."

Azure glanced over her shoulder, surprised to find Harper holding a small red gift bag in his outstretched hands. "What is it?"

"Open it and see."

As she reached for the bag, her hands skimmed Harper's fingers. Lust engulfed her, caused her body to burn hotter than the tip of a flame. All night, they'd danced and flirted and held hands, and now Azure was so desperate for Harper all she could think about was making love to him on the satin-draped bed. She wanted to kiss him, to use her lips and mouth and hands to convey what she was feeling inside, but she knew Harper would reject her. And that would kill her. She'd been rejected by her peers, her family and enough men to last a lifetime, and Azure wasn't going to risk her pride for a few fleeting moments of pleasure.

"Harper, it's beautiful," she whispered, taking the white lace nightgown out of the bag.

"It's for your trousseau," he explained. "You don't have to put it on, but I made a big show of buying it this afternoon at that boutique you went to, so you might as well keep it."

Azure didn't know what to say, so she remained silent. It was either that or throw herself in his arms and devour his lips. But since she wasn't a soap star, and he wasn't her leading man, she forced her gaze away from his mouth and prayed for an extra dose of self-control.

"I wanted you to have something to remember tonight."

"You mean, I don't get to keep my wedding ring?" Azure exclaimed, holding her left hand up high in the air and wiggling her fourth finger. "I never imagined myself getting married, but this is the ring of my dreams!"

"After the performance you gave tonight, you deserve to

keep it. You were amazing, Azure, and charmed everyone from my brothers to my cynical cousins. My family loves you, and I think our plan is off to a great start."

"You do? I don't know, Harper. Your mom is awfully upset about us getting married."

Harper loosened his tie and unbuttoned his tuxedo jacket. Taking it off, he draped it over the back of the cushioned desk chair. "Don't worry about my mom. She'll come around."

Yeah, when she's standing over my casket, Azure thought, chilled by the frightening image that flashed in her mind. Feeling Harper's eyes on her, she feigned interest in the framed art on the walls and moved toward the fireplace. On the mantel, scented candles, vases filled with dried flowers and glass sculptures were artfully arranged, and gave Azure something to do besides ogling Harper. Standing beside him was too much. Too much pressure, too much temptation. What if he tried to kiss her? A more troubling thought struck. What if he didn't?

"You go off to bed," Harper said, putting his arm around her shoulder and steering her toward the master bedroom. "I'll see you in the morning."

"Where are you going to sleep?"

"I'll take the couch."

"Oh, okay. Good night."

Harper gave Azure a chaste kiss on the cheek, then closed the bedroom door.

An hour later, Azure lay in the king-size bed alone, showered, changed and unable to sleep. She tossed and turned, like a woman with a heavy conscience, and debated turning on the TV to keep her company. Azure heard a phone ring. Her curiosity piqued, she listened intently for several moments. When she heard Harper's voice, she sat up in bed. Azure knew it was wrong to spy—it was one of the ten commandments of journalism or something—but she threw off her covers and dashed across the room before guilt kicked in.

Opening the door a crack, she pressed her body flat against the wall and peeked inside the living room. Harper was standing beside the entertainment unit, clad in nothing but black pajama bottoms, talking on his cell phone. He was speaking to a woman! Had to be. Why else would he be whispering? His tone was soft, as warm and tender as the kiss he'd given her at the altar, and when he chuckled, his eyes twinkled brighter than the stars in the sky.

"I know, and I understand, the ceremony took everyone by surprise," she overheard Harper say. "We'll get together next week. I'll free up time in my schedule to make it happen...."

Backing away from the door, Azure swallowed the hard, painful lump in her throat that threatened to choke her dead. *What do I care? What Harper does after dark is his business.* Her words provided no comfort and didn't stop her eyes from tearing up.

There are some things smart, savvy women just don't do, Azure thought, shaking her head in self-disgust. *Like entering wet T-shirt contests or shaving off their eyebrows and penciling them in. And intelligent chicks never,* ever *enter sham unions with men who look and sound and smell like Harper Hamilton.* Azure's stomach churned violently as she struggled to control her emotions, to come to terms with the colossal mistake she'd made just to advance her career.

Slumping down on the bed, Azure slapped away the tears coursing down her cheeks. "This is what I get for marrying a guy on the rebound," she said, overcome with feelings of regret and despair. "I can't believe I agreed to something so stupid!"

More tears came. They spilled down her face, splashed like raindrops onto the white, lace-trimmed nightgown Harper had given her. Azure needed a cold drink, preferably something with alcohol in it, but her vision was so blurry she couldn't see where the minibar was. It didn't matter. Azure wasn't sticking around. She had to leave, had to get the hell out of the honeymoon suite. Marrying Harper was a mistake, but it wasn't too late to put an end to the charade.

"Azure, are you still awake? I'm sorry to bother you, but your cell—"

Cringing inwardly, she shielded her tear-streaked face with her hands. She'd left the bedroom door open, and now Harper was standing in the doorway, staring at her. He wore a sympathetic face, one touched with care and concern, and was holding her cell phone in his outstretched hands. Azure watched as he placed it on the dresser and strode across the room toward her. Feeling like a big, fat crybaby, she lowered her gaze to the plush, carpeted floor. Azure wiped her cheeks with the back of her hand, but when Harper sat down beside her on the bed, she wanted to dive under the covers and cry some more. "I'm fine, Harper. You can go."

"You left your cell phone on one of the end tables," he explained, his voice a degree lower, softer than usual. "It's been ringing off the hook, and when I saw your parents' name flash on the screen, I decided to bring it to you. They probably heard about our wedding on the news and want to congratulate us."

"I doubt it," she murmured, her head low, her shoulders bent.

"Is that why you're crying? Because you think your parents are upset?"

Azure pretended not to hear the question.

"Talk to me," he urged, taking her hand and cradling it gently in his palm.

She studied the carpet, the pattern on the bedsheet, the intricate flower detail along the helm of her nightgown. Azure looked everywhere but at Harper, and the more he caressed her hands, the more embarrassed she felt. Why did he have to come in here? Why couldn't he have just stayed in the living room and let her cry in peace?

"Did I do something wrong?"

"This is so humiliating."

"You have nothing to be embarrassed about, Azure. Sometimes after a long, stressful day I go home and have a good cry, too."

A smile tickled her lips. Harper was trying to make her laugh, trying to lighten the mood, and the tactic worked. Her tears dried up, her breathing slowed and her heart quit pounding. He caressed her hands, slowly, with such tenderness she almost cried out. And that would have made her look desperate. But deep down, that's exactly what she was. Desperate for a man she'd been fantasizing about since high school.

"Do you want me to take you home?"

"What if someone sees us? They'll think there's trouble in paradise."

"Is there?"

Azure stared at Harper, and when he met her gaze, she decided to ask him about his late-night phone call. "Was that your ex on the phone?"

Surprise showed on his face. "No, it was Marissa. She called to apologize for leaving the reception early. I told her not to sweat it, but she promised to make it up to me by having us over for dinner one day next week. What made you think it was my ex-girlfriend?"

"Don't you mean your *ex-fiancée?*"

"I never proposed. She did."

"But you said yes."

Harper nodded. "It seemed like the right thing to do, but if I could do it all over again, I would have said no. Women aren't supposed to propose to men and—"

"Why not?" Azure asked, frowning at him. "I guess you've

never heard the saying 'A man chases a woman until *she* catches him'!"

"Call me old-fashioned, but I just don't think it's right. Men like to be in control, or at least think they are, and a sister down on bended knee, popping the question to her man, looks as awkward as a Liza Minnelli kiss."

Azure cracked up, laughed until there were tears in her eyes, but this time she didn't feel like the biggest fool to ever walk the face of the earth. She felt relaxed, at ease, and was glad Harper was sitting beside her, cracking jokes. Azure only wished he was wearing a T-shirt or, better yet, a turtleneck sweater. Her gaze kept sliding down his chest, and every time her eyes landed on his nipples, she lost her train of thought. It was a struggle to concentrate on what he was saying, a fight, more challenging than that Tae Bo class she did last week at the gym.

"I hope you'll take me up on my offer and accompany me to Cabo San Lucas for Christmas," Harper said, giving her hand a soft, affectionate squeeze before releasing it. "You came through big-time for me tonight, and I want to do something special for you."

"You've already done enough. You paid for my dress, the reception, this suite."

"Tonight was some night, huh?"

Azure smiled at the memory of their first kiss, and all the sensual slow dances they'd shared over the night. She craved his touch and was so hungry for his kiss it was all she could think about. Scared she was going to act on her impulses, Azure inched over on the bed to create more personal space, and clasped her wayward hands together.

"When I saw you coming down the aisle, I thought I was going to pass out," he confessed, wearing a boyish smile. "You took my breath away, and I couldn't have been more proud that you were my bride."

Her heart stilled. It was difficult to remain upright when Harper was stroking her arms. Her legs quivered like Jell-O, and the silky hue of his tone whipped her horny body into a frenzy.

Passion built.

Rose to devastating heights.

The air was filled with the perfume of her desire, flowing through the master bedroom like a mighty rushing wind. Their eyes connected, held for a beat and then Harper kissed her. His lips moved against hers, captured them in a dizzying, mind-numbing hold. Azure felt his hands in her hair, on her check, caressing her neck and shoulders. They collapsed onto the bed, panting, moaning, delirious with an explosive, unquenchable lust.

Harper cupped her breasts through her nightgown, flicked and massaged and kneaded until her nipples hardened. Lost in the sensual whirlwind of his kiss, Azure gripped his shoulders, held on to him for dear life. *Don't stop...please don't stop...*.

Azure was hot, overcome, ready to get on top of Harper and ride him to oblivion, but she resisted the urge to take control. She had to let him lead, had to let him dictate the pace. Being in his arms was a dream come true, and for the first time in Azure's life she wanted to throw caution to the wind and act out her secret fantasy. Right now, tonight, in the middle of the king-size bed. Azure didn't ever want the kiss to end, and when Harper started to pull away, disappointment rained down on her.

"I crossed the line. I'm sorry."

Sorry? His words were a slap in the face, but Azure masked her pain by feigning indifference. "Harper, it's no big deal. We both had a lot to drink tonight."

"I don't know what got into me."

Harper lowered his head, ran a hand over his close-cropped

hair. He looked pained, as if he'd just stubbed his toe on the edge of the bed, and a scowl was stretched across his thick, juicy lips. Lips Azure wished she was still kissing and licking and sucking.

"Forget about it," she said with a dismissive wave of her hand. "I know I have."

Harper shot to his feet, took a giant step away from the bed. "I'm a man of my word, and I promise I'll never do anything that impulsive or irresponsible again."

Azure couldn't put her thoughts into words. Her emotions were all over the place, as scattered as a woman battling menopause, and Azure feared if she spoke she would break down again. And Harper finding her crying in bed once was humiliating enough.

"I better get out of here and let you get some rest. The next few days are going to be insanely busy for us and—"

"They are?"

Harper nodded, seemed to relax as he discussed their plans for the upcoming week. "My aunt and uncle are expecting us at the Integrity Estate for Sunday brunch, and you're going to have to be on your game, because they're probably going to grill you about our relationship."

"That's to be expected. Before tonight, they had no idea we were a couple. Will your mom…I mean, will your parents be there, as well?"

"No, they never go to Sunday brunch."

Azure swallowed a cheer. The fewer interactions she had with Mrs. Hamilton, the better, and if that meant avoiding her mother-in-law for the next three months, that's just what she'd do.

"On Wednesday, we have a fitting at Haute Couture for my aunt Jeanette's charity ball next month, and I have a few interviews lined up for us on Thursday and Friday morning."

"Wow, you weren't kidding. We *are* going to be busy."

Azure yawned, then wore a sheepish smile. "See, just listening to you is making me tired!"

"All right, all right, I get the hint." Chuckling, Harper bent down, and gave her a chaste kiss on the cheek. "Good night, Azure. Sleep well."

Azure nodded, watched helplessly as he strode out of the bedroom. She didn't want Harper to leave; she wanted him to stay and keep her company. After all, it was their honeymoon. Sure, their wedding ceremony was all for show, but the kisses they'd shared tonight had stirred some very powerful feelings inside her. Feelings that filled every inch of her with desire. *I'm in way over my head,* Azure thought, peering into the living room to catch another glimpse of Harper. *And something tells me things are only going to go downhill from here.*

Chapter 12

"Girrllll, you're lookin' hot, and those snakeskin pumps are a killer!"

Azure tossed a look over her shoulder, and when she saw *Eminence* magazine's voluptuous, dark-skinned beauty editor sashaying down the hall toward her, she waved in greeting. It was the first time she'd seen Bridgett Dalton since marrying Harper last week, and although she was in a hurry, she didn't want to be rude by rushing off.

"Thanks, Bridgett! My husband bought them for me," Azure said, resisting the urge to do the happy dance right then and there. She was Mrs. Harper Hamilton, and so thrilled to be married to such a thoughtful, generous man, she wanted to shout it the rooftops. "My man has great taste, doesn't he?"

Her coworker stuck out her pierced tongue. "Show-off!"

The women laughed.

"How are you doing, Bridgett? I haven't seen you in ages."

"That's because you've been busy setting up house with

that fine-ass attorney," she quipped, swiveling her neck. "I was stunned when I heard Harper Hamilton had finally tied the knot, and when I saw your wedding photo flash on my TV screen, I dropped my cappuccino!"

Azure giggled.

"I had no clue you guys were dating, and if I had, I probably would have slashed your tires in a jealous rage, because I've had a crush on that man for years!"

You and me both, girl. You and me both, Azure thought, closing her office door. Clutching her cell phone in her hand, she heaved her purse over her shoulder with the other and moved briskly down the hall toward the sun-drenched lobby. Bridgett was hot on her heels, questioning her about the intimate details of her whirlwind romance with Harper and chatting a mile a minute.

"Harper sounds like a really great guy, but you better be careful, girl. He *is* a Hamilton."

Slanting her head in her colleague's direction, she shot Bridgett an incredulous, what-are-you-talking-about look. "What's that supposed to mean?"

"I'm just saying, when it comes to the ladies his father, Frank, has quite the reputation, and you know what they say, 'The apple doesn't fall far from the tree.'"

Azure slowed but didn't stop. She had no idea what Bridgett was talking about but decided not to question her further. On any other day, she'd join her loquacious coworker in the staff room for a cup of coffee and some juicy celebrity gossip, but today Azure didn't have time to shoot the breeze. She had to hustle if she was going to make it to Haute Couture by four o'clock. The entire Hamilton family was going to be fitted for next month's charity ball at the by-appointment-only boutique, and Azure shuddered to think what Harper's mother would do to her if she was late.

"Let's get together for drinks one day next week," Bridgett

proposed when they reached the reception desk. "Give me a call tomorrow and we'll set something up."

Azure jabbed the elevator button. "Sounds like a plan. Talk to you later!"

The elevator doors slid open, and Azure groaned inwardly. People were crammed inside the box like human crayons. Sliding between two middle-aged men yakking on their respective cell phones, Azure hoped and prayed the ride would be a painless one. Pop music blared from someone's headphones, and the stench of cologne, nicotine and a day's worth of sweat was so heavy in the air Azure's stomach lurched. But before she could jump out, the doors closed, sealing her inside the tight, putrid-smelling space.

Azure felt her cell phone vibrate and checked the number on the screen. It was her mom. Again. She had been dodging her mother since the day after the wedding, and had yet to respond to any calls or text messages. Her parents were upset she'd gone off and married Harper, and rightly so, but Azure didn't have the energy to deal with them today. Not after the long, stressful day she'd had.

Azure thought of switching off her cell, but she was expecting a call from Demetri Morretti's publicist and was so anxious to find out if the baseball superstar would grant her request for an interview, she'd been clutching her BlackBerry in her right hand all day.

The phone stopped ringing, then started up again seconds later. Azure pretended not to hear it, but when the silver-haired woman beside her shot her an evil look, she reluctantly answered the phone. "Hey, Mom, how are you—"

"Alice Rose Ellison, are you out of your ever-loving mind?"

The elevator went quiet, and Azure could feel the heat of a dozen stares.

"Mom, I can't talk right now—"

"Why the hell not?"

Azure stared down at the phone. *Uh-oh, she's really mad.*

"Imagine my surprise when I turned on my computer and saw your wedding pictures splashed across the society section of the *Philadelphia Blaze!*"

"I can explain...."

"What were you thinking?" she demanded, her tone colder than ice.

"I wasn't. Everything happened so fast, and I got caught up in the moment, I guess."

"Thank God you did! Marrying Harper Hamilton was the best decision you ever made."

Azure sputtered, tripped over her tongue in her haste to make sense of what her mother was saying. "So, you're not angry that I married Harper?"

"No, of course not. Harper Hamilton is the ultimate catch. Rich, successful, well connected. You couldn't have done any better, honey. Well done. Nicely played."

Azure frowned. "I don't understand. Are you mad at me or not?"

"I'm not mad that you married Harper Hamilton. I'm mad that you married him in that hideous-looking satin dress!"

Of course, Azure thought, shaking her head. *I should have known.*

"I mean, really, Alice, what were you thinking? Why would you set out to be the butt of Perez Hilton's vicious jokes?"

Azure heard giggles and chuckles behind her, and knew everyone in the elevator was enjoying the show. Hanging up on her mom would be disrespectful, and Azure knew her dad was probably waiting in the wings to speak to her, but she had to get off the phone before she lost her cool and said something she'd later regret.

"Honey, you really need to get a gym membership and sign up for one of their advanced cardio classes. If you exercise for an hour every day and stick to a strict, eight-hundred-calorie diet, those love handles will be gone before you know it."

Azure winced. Even Mrs. Hamilton wasn't *that* mean.

The elevators slid open, and Azure gulped in some fresh air. "Mom, I'll call you later," she lied, hustling through the lobby and flagging down a taxi once outside. "I'm on my way to Haute Couture and I really can't talk right now."

"Why not?" she barked, her tone losing its warmth. "Are you having a second, more extravagant wedding ceremony? One you're planning to exclude your loving family from?"

"No, Mom, I have to find a dress for the Hamilton family charity gala."

"Oh yes, yes, their annual fundraiser for the Tuck Me In Foundation. I went a few years back and enjoyed myself immensely. Whatever you do, don't buy anything white or strapless or satin. It will only emphasize how big your butt is. And those pesky love handles."

Azure's thumb inched toward the end button.

"And one last thing, make sure you get two seats at Mayor Nutter's table."

"Mom, Harper and I will be sitting with the rest of the family at—"

"The tickets aren't for you, honey. They're for me and Dad."

Azure gulped. "You're coming to Philly next month?"

"You bet your stiletto boots we are!" her mom shrieked, her voice high-pitched, loud and excited. "I mean, really, Alice, what kind of mother would I be if I didn't come to town to meet my wealthy new son-in-law and his *über*-rich family?"

A mother who wanted to spare her already stressed-out daughter any more humiliation, Azure thought, blowing out a breath of frustration. Now she had to contend with Mrs. Hamilton *and* her mother at next month's charity gala. The thought made her stomach churn, and even thinking about

Harper didn't help. With Harper, she was free to be her insecure, sarcastic self, and knowing that he liked her—faults and all—usually was enough to turn her smile upside down. But not today. Not in light of the bombshell her mother had just dropped.

"Ta-ta, dear. Now run along and go get those tickets. Talk to you soon!"

When Azure heard the dial tone buzz in her ear, she clicked off her phone and hurled it inside her purse. A taxi stopped, and she ducked inside.

Dropping her purse at her feet, she slumped in the backseat and closed her tear-filled eyes. Azure didn't know if she was feeling emotional because of the hurtful things her mother had said, because she was exhausted or both. She couldn't stop thinking about the charity gala, couldn't stop thinking about all the things that could go wrong at the Hamilton family fundraiser. With her mother *and* mother-in-law there, the event was sure to be a fiasco, an evening filled with tension, stress and more drama than a daytime soap opera.

And Azure had a feeling she was going to be smack-dab in the middle of all the chaos. *Does the man upstairs really have it out for me or what?*

"Oh my goodness…." The words tumbled out of Azure's mouth when Harper emerged from behind the changing room door in a tailored black tuxedo. Her eyes stalked him through the boutique, and when he joined his brothers on the raised, circular stage in front of the mirror, Azure felt her girly parts throb and tingle. *Thank God I'm sitting or I would have fainted at his feet!*

Licking her dry lips, she fanned a hand in front of her face. It was stunning, mind-boggling actually. Azure had never met a family like the Hamiltons. Not only had Philadelphia's wealthiest African-American family been blessed with good looks; they'd been endowed with smarts, intelligence and winning personalities. The Hamilton clan shared a tight bond, one that Azure noticed the moment she entered Harper's uncle's estate, and watching Harper joke around with his brothers and cousins made Azure wish she and Eden were closer.

Azure heard someone groan, and turned around just in time to see Marissa Hamilton collapse onto one of the plush beige chairs. "Are you okay?" she asked gently, noting the attorney's pale skin and lifeless disposition. "No offense, but you don't look too good."

She combed a hand through her long, tussled brown hair. "I'll be okay. It's just the flu. I've survived a lot worse."

"Do you want me to get you something to drink?" Azure gestured to the round glass table beside the front window. "They have everything here. Coffee, tea, soda."

"No, thanks. I've already had three cans of ginger ale! I'm going to sneak out of here when my mom's not looking and go home to bed. I was at the office until midnight, and up by six for court, so I didn't get much sleep last night."

I know just how you feel, Azure thought, wearing a sympathetic smile. Tossing and turning had become her new late-night pastime. She hadn't had a good night sleep since moving into Harper's sprawling Society Hill home, and Azure wondered how many more sleepless nights she could take before collapsing from sheer exhaustion.

"This is my big break!" Keeping her eyes glued to her mother, who was chatting on her cell phone and fussing with her husband's pin-striped tie, Marissa quickly collected her things and sprang to her feet. "Bye, Azure. See you soon!"

Alone now, Azure returned to doing what she did best: lusting after Harper. That's why she couldn't sleep. They lived in separate wings of the house, but Azure was very much aware of his presence and knew his daily routine like the back of her hand. She wasn't a morning person and struggled to make it to work on time every day, but the second she heard Harper in the kitchen, she jumped out of bed. After freshening up, Azure joined him at the breakfast bar, and there, over mugs of freshly brewed coffee and cinnamon bagels, they discussed their plans for the day and which high-profile events to attend in and around town.

"How do I look?"

Azure blinked, and when she saw Harper stalking toward her, wearing a boyish smile, she had to stop herself from leaping off the couch and straight into his arms. Harper kept his physique in tip-top shape by playing racquetball five days a week, and as her gaze spilled down his chest, Azure decided he had the sexiest body she'd ever seen. "You look beautiful! Like a Calvin Klein model ripping the runway!"

Harper's brothers—Benjamin and Shawn—erupted in laughter. They stood on the raised stage, in front of the mirror, elbowing each other like a bunch of middle school boys watching a couple round third base under the football bleachers.

Harper chuckled. "I'm not beautiful. I'm tough and manly and macho."

"Well, I think you're gorgeous," she said, admiring his physique, "and anyone who thinks differently is probably legally blind!"

More hearty chuckles from the well-dressed peanut gallery.

"I don't know about you, Cupcake, but I'm ready to call it a day," Harper said, sitting down beside Azure on the plush sofa and resting a hand on her thigh.

Azure knew Harper was only touching her for show, only playing the role of the loving, affectionate husband, but every time Harper touched her, she melted. His gentle caress ignited her desires, and when he gave her a peck on the lips, her body shook like a rattle.

"We should go for dinner at Table 13 once we finish up here."

Azure agreed. She'd been on her feet for the past hour, had been poked and pinched by the seamstress as she modeled the black, one-shoulder dress she was wearing to next month's charity gala and was so hungry she was beginning to feel faint. And after being interrogated by Harper's father, Frank, about their relationship, she could use a tall, cold cocktail. "Is it safe for us to leave?" Azure asked, glancing around the boutique in search of Harper's bossy, high-strung aunt. The wife and mother of three was not only planning the upcoming charity fundraiser, but giving a speech, as well, and she insisted that everyone look chic and sophisticated for the event.

"Everyone's been fitted, so it should be fine."

"Your mom's not coming?"

Harper shook his head. "No, she's home sick with the flu."

Azure wondered if Mrs. Hamilton was actually sick or just avoiding her. The thought made guilt rain down on her, made her feel as if she was somehow responsible for her mother-in-law's frame of mind. She was only married to Harper for show, but Azure didn't want to cause a rift between mother and son. Maybe she should try and reach out to Mrs. Hamilton. Make an effort to smooth things over with her. *I'll send her flowers and a box of chocolates,* Azure decided, feeling confident about her decision. *If that doesn't score me a few points, I don't know what will!* "I hope your mom feels better soon."

"I phoned her a couple hours ago, and she actually sounded pretty good," Harper said with a smooth nod. "I'm sure she'll be up and running in no time."

"Does your aunt Jeanette know your mom's not coming? She was looking around for her a few minutes ago."

"Yeah, I told her. She's flipping out, but I told her not to worry. There's still plenty of time for my mom to get fitted. Hell, she's a designer. She can do her own alterations!"

"Why didn't your mom design the outfits for the charity gala?" Azure asked, her curiosity getting the best of her. "She's the latest 'It' designer, and the whole fashion world is buzzing about her fall collection."

Harper shrugged. "I don't know. These days Mom's insanely busy, and I'm guessing she probably couldn't fit it into her already-tight schedule."

"Has your mom always worked?"

"Yes. She did a great job juggling everything, and I can't ever remember a time in my life when she wasn't there for me or didn't put me and my brothers first."

"I envy you. My mother never worked, so she made me— or rather me losing weight—her full-time job. She used to force me to exercise every day before and after school. To this day, I hate spandex *and* Richard Simmons."

Harper gave her knee a light squeeze. "You're not alone, Azure. I had an overbearing parent, too. My mom was around so much I used to forget she even had a job!"

They shared a laugh, but when Harper spoke again, his voice was filled with admiration.

"My mom was the best. Loving, warm and a lot of fun. My dad was always off working, so she had to pick up the slack, which I'm sure was no easy feat. You've met my brothers," he said, raising his eyebrows. "They're a handful! Especially that Nelson!"

Listening to Harper talk about his childhood made Azure wonder what it would be like having a family with him. It was never going to happen, but she daydreamed about what their children would look like. Harper would be a great dad, the best. He'd be strict, but loving, compassionate and attentive. And if they had a girl, he'd probably spoil her rotten. She'd be a daddy's little girl for sure, nipping at his heels all day long. Harper would love their daughter unconditionally, no matter what. He wouldn't be ashamed to take her out in public, the way her father had been with her.

Azure fiddled with her purse strap as painful childhood memories engulfed her. A thick, acrid taste filled her dry mouth. Wiping her mind clean didn't expunge her feelings of bitterness, but when Harper leaned over and kissed her, her scowl morphed into a smile.

"I'm going to change, and then we'll get out of here, okay?"

Azure nodded, and as she watched Harper stride back across the boutique, she undressed all six feet two inches of him with her eyes. Staring up at the ceiling, she prayed for an extra dose of self-control, because these days keeping her hands to herself and off Harper was more challenging than deciphering the lyrics to a Nicki Minaj song.

Chapter 13

"Just one more question before I let you two lovebirds go," the bubbly, rail-thin Channel Six TV news reporter said, raising her index finger in the air, "This question was posted on our Facebook page from one of our loyal viewers, and I'm *very* curious to hear your response. Are you guys thinking of starting a family anytime soon?"

"No!"

"Yes!"

Azure cranked her neck in Harper's direction. The bright studio lights illuminated the twinkle in his eyes, and a grin was playing on his full lips. He was enjoying the interview, and discussing their sham of a marriage had put him in a fun, playful mood. This was the third interview they'd done today, and although Harper had said several things that surprised her during the segment, his response to the baby question left Azure at a loss for words.

"I want to have kids right away, and we're having a hell of a good time practicing!"

Coughing, Azure rubbed a hand over her pounding chest. An oversize fan was blowing cool air into the studio, but sweat drenched her palms and the back of her white ruffled blouse. Azure wanted to interrupt, to stop Harper from saying anything else outrageous, but she feared if she opened her mouth gibberish would fall out.

Blown away by Harper's uncharacteristic display of bravado, Azure listened in stunned disbelief as he told the gregarious TV host—and 1.5 million viewers—how much fun they were having in the bedroom.

"Life is good," Harper said, staring straight into the camera. "I honestly can't remember the last time I was this happy."

"I bet," quipped the host. "You look like one *very* satiated man to me!"

He chuckled, agreed wholeheartedly. "I'm looking forward to the next chapter of our lives, and I just know Azure is going to be an incredible mother. She's intelligent and witty and she never fails to make me laugh." Gazing at her, he rested a hand on her leg, slowly caressed her thigh. Harper wore a devilish smile, one that should be illegal in all fifty states, and when he leaned over and pecked Azure on the lips, she swallowed a moan.

"I know you guys are newlyweds," the host joked, holding her hands up in the air, "but slow your roll. This is daytime TV!"

The studio audience giggled and cheered.

Azure blew out a breath, shifted around on the plush beige couch. Global warming had to be to blame for her out-of-control body temperature. That or her flesh was reacting to Harper's innocent caress. Which made no sense. This wasn't the first time he'd touched her or stared deep into her eyes. But maybe that was it. Maybe the more he touched her, the harder it was for her to stay in control. Maybe? Azure wanted to laugh. There were no ifs, ands or buts about it. She craved him—his kiss, his touch, the feel of his hands between her legs—and like an addict, she couldn't wait for her next fix.

"I can't wait for Azure to get pregnant. I plan to take extra good care of her and…"

Azure felt as if a hypnotist had put her in a trance. She couldn't stop staring at Harper, couldn't stop picturing them in bed making love. They were never going to produce the love child he spoke so fondly of, but Azure was all for a night or two of carnal pleasure.

"We'd like to have at least four kids, so if you'll excuse us, we really must go, because we have some baby making to do!"

"Well, there you have it, folks," the host said, wearing a cheeky smile. "They're hard at work making babies!"

Shrieks of excitement and applause filled the air.

"I want to thank Philadelphia's newest sweethearts, Harper and Azure Hamilton, for stopping by *City Spotlight* this morning," the host said, staring straight into the camera. "It's been fun. Come back and visit us real soon."

"Thanks for having us," Harper said with a nod to the host and one to the studio audience. "And we look forward to seeing you and your wonderful viewers at the Tuck Me In Foundation charity gala next month."

"I'll be there with bells on!" the host said. "After the commercial break, we'll be joined by rising pop star Treasure J and celebrity chef Chaz Murano. Stay tuned!"

When the cameras stopped rolling, crew members swarmed the set. Lights were repositioned, furniture was moved and the statuesque producer hustled around the room, flapping her hands and shouting orders to her ten-man crew.

"Azure, you were great. The cameras loved you!" Reaching over, Harper unclipped her microphone and handed it to the engineer. Standing, he clasped her hand and helped her up from the couch. Intertwining his fingers with hers, he caressed his thumb over her soft, warm flesh. Holding her gaze, he raised her hand to his mouth and kissed it. "You're the best thing that ever happened to me. You know that, right?"

"I feel the same way."

Azure cast a glance around the room and noticed all the women on set were shooting her evil daggers. No surprise. They thought she was legitimately married to Harper, a hot, rich attorney who came from money, and Azure didn't blame them for wishing her dead.

"Are you okay? You're shaking."

Harper wrapped her up in his arms, cradling her to his chest.

A delicious warmth flowed through her. Harper's touch aroused her, caused her to melt in his arms. It had been like that from day one. In public, he was a loving, doting husband, more excited than an A-list actor jumping on Oprah's couch. And Azure enjoyed every wonderful minute of it. She loved the attention, how desirable Harper made her feel, and all the thoughtful things he did to brighten her day. On Sunday, he took her to the opera, yesterday he'd treated her to a shopping spree at Barney's and tonight he was taking her to see a comedy show. Their first two weeks of marriage had been a dream, one filled with laughs, kisses and plenty of tender moments, but it was getting harder and harder for Azure to separate fact from fiction.

"Where to?"

Azure blinked, shrugged. "I don't know. Are you going in to the office?"

"That depends on whether or not you're free." Harper smiled. "To be honest, I wasn't planning on it, so I cleared my schedule for the day."

"But you have that big fraud case to prep for."

"I know, but I'd much rather spend some quality time with you."

"What did you have in mind?"

His gaze zeroed in on her lips. "You don't want to know."

"But I do—" Azure paused when she spotted a stunning, fair-skinned creature sashay toward them and tap Harper on the shoulder.

"Harper, it's so good to see you. How have you been?"

"Vienna? What are you doing here?"

Azure felt his muscles tense. Stepping back, he tightened his hold around her waist and angled his body toward the door. As if he was plotting his escape.

"Treasure J is my newest client," she explained, gesturing to the adorable girl in the pink denim outfit practicing dance moves on the circular stage. "Mark my words. Treasure J is going to explode onto the music scene and knock Taylor Swift off the charts!"

Harper gave a cold, bitter laugh, one that would scare a villain in a horror movie. "You're hardly one to be advising impressionable young girls."

"Be nice," she sang, tilting her head to the side and propping her hands on her hips. "Remember, I know all your secrets, Harper, and if you're mean to me, I'll go to the media—"

"Bye, Vienna. Have a nice life."

"Aren't you going to introduce me to your blushing new bride?"

Harper hesitated, then gave a slow nod. "Azure, this is Vienna Abrams. An old friend."

"Okay, Harper, I'll let you tell it," she quipped, rolling her eyes to the ceiling, "but 'friends' don't plan an elaborate destination wedding."

Azure froze. So, this was his ex. The woman Harper had planned to marry. Jealousy reared its ugly head, caused Azure to feel insecure and inferior in the music executive's presence. Vienna was just Harper's type. Tall, curvy, with a perfect hourglass figure. She didn't have an ounce of fat anywhere, or pesky love handles to contend with, either.

"It's a pleasure to meet you, Azure, and I hope you and Harper have a long and happy marriage. All the best to you both!"

Azure didn't know what to say. She wasn't expecting this, wasn't expecting Harper's ex to be so kind and gracious. Vienna sounded sincere, as though she meant every word, and was wearing a friendly expression on her pretty, oval-shaped face. Azure tried to smile, but it felt as if her mouth was wired shut. "Thanks," she managed after a long, tense moment.

"Azure, baby, we better get going."

With that, Harper led her across the room, out the studio doors and into the sleek black town car idling at the curb. Azure didn't mind the rush. The quicker she got away from Harper's ex, the better, because meeting the woman Harper had planned to marry—not for publicity or fame, but for love—was more than Azure could bear.

On Friday evening, Azure walked into Harper's gourmet kitchen fully expecting to see his Persian-born housekeeper behind the stove, but instead found Harper stirring a black oversize pot with a silver spoon. The grill was sizzling, the round, glass table was set for two and a cool, crisp breeze blew in through the bay window.

Rap music pumped out of the living room stereo, and to her surprise, Harper was rhyming fluently to the track playing. He was bobbing his head, rocking his hard, muscled body to the strong, pulsing beat.

Azure's thoughts took an explicit detour. As she watched Harper, two things struck her at once: how damn good he looked in his V-neck sweater and faded blue jeans and how much she enjoyed seeing this side to him. This sexy, laid-back side.

"I can't believe you're home," she said, unzipping her jacket and placing it on the armrest of the leather sectional couch. Everything in Harper's Society Hill home was luxurious, opulent and beautifully arranged, and when their marriage was over, Azure knew she'd have a hard time leaving Harper's lavish, six-bedroom house. "You never get home before six, but it's only four-thirty. Is everything okay?"

"Yeah, fine, I just decided to quit a little early today."

Azure didn't believe Harper for a minute, but she knew he wasn't going to tell her the truth. Not that she needed him to. He'd been acting strange ever since they ran into Vienna at the TV studio, and after three days of his moody behavior, she'd finally decided to quit asking him what was wrong. If Harper didn't want to talk to her, fine, she'd just do her own thing tonight. "Okay, I guess I'll see you later. I'm going upstairs to work on my next article."

"Are you hungry?"

"Not really. I stopped by the condo after work to see my cats and had a slice of Maggie's homemade apple pie." Azure sniffed the air. The kitchen smelled like cumin, and although she'd just eaten a sweet, gooey dessert, the spicy scent aroused her hunger.

"I wanted to do something special for you, so I made dinner."

"But you don't cook."

"True, but I make a *mean* peppercorn steak," he said, wearing a proud smile. "One bite, and you'll be singing my praises."

"What else is on the menu, Home Boyardee?"

Chuckling, he put down the spoon and lowered the temperature on the stove. "Caesar salad, French bread and wild rice."

"And for dessert?"

"Chocolate cupcakes."

Sighing dramatically, she tilted her head to the side and placed a hand on her chest. "A man after my heart."

"You sound pleased," he said, uncorking the wine bottle on the counter. "Does that mean you'll join me for dinner? Please say yes. I hate eating alone."

"Sure, why not? It's the least I can do since you went to all this trouble."

"Great! Hang tight. Dinner will be ready in ten minutes."

Azure picked up the CD lying on the granite counter, flipped it over and scanned the song titles. "I didn't know you liked rap music."

"Who doesn't?" he joked, stealing her favorite line. "I've been a hip-hop fan ever since high school, and after I heard 'Fight the Power' by Public Enemy, I wanted to be a rapper!"

"I'm guessing that didn't go over too well with your parents."

"You're right about that."

"Did they confiscate your boom box or ground you for a month?"

"Both. My dad was so angry he tossed my stereo out the window and all the rap CDs I'd saved up to buy!" Harper chuckled at the memory. "It's in my blood to be an attorney, to practice and study law, but I've always wished I could work with artists and actors, too."

"Then why not start your own law practice and specialize in the entertainment field? You're an accomplished attorney, with an impeccable reputation, and I bet you'd have celebrities lined up to sign with you in no time."

"I've been thinking of starting my own practice for a while now. It's just an idea, something I've been pondering off and on for the last year," he confessed. "My family wouldn't take the news well, especially my dad, but I know over time he'd come around."

"I think you should go for it." Azure reached into the fruit basket, plucked a grape off the vine and popped it into her mouth. "And if you name your law firm something cool and catchy like Hit Makers and Associates, rappers will come running when they're in trouble with the law!"

Harper tossed his head back and gave a long, hearty chuckle. "You're too much."

"That's why you love me!" Azure winced when the words left her mouth. Sometimes she didn't know when to stop. Shaking her head, she shook off her comment with a wave of her hand. "I'm just kidding, Harper. You know me. I'll do anything for a laugh."

"Anything?"

Harper picked up the credit-card-size remote control and pointed it at the entertainment unit. The lights dimmed, the blinds opened, revealing a stunning view of the landscape and the rap music was replaced with cool jazz. Harper picked up the bottle of wine, filled two flutes and handed one to Azure. "You will always have a special place in my heart, always be someone I care deeply for, and I wish you nothing but the best in life."

Azure lowered her glass from her lips. "Why does this sound like goodbye?"

"Because it is." Harper blew out a ragged breath, raked a hand over his head. "Azure, I'm sorry. I know we had an agreement, but I can't do this anymore. You can't live here."

"Is this about my dirty clothes piled up in the laundry room?" she asked, resting her glass on the counter. "I'll get to it tonight, I promise, as soon as we finish dinner."

"This is not about the laundry. You've been a model room-mate."

Azure felt her shoulders slump, but she didn't crumble. She would put on a brave front, remain unaffected and aloof, even if it killed her. And Azure didn't doubt that it would.

Like a fool, she'd foolishly believed that over time Harper might come to feel something for her. *I should have known this day was coming,* she thought, overcome by the weight of her sadness, *Harper Hamilton is, and always will be, out of my league.*

"If you want, I can help you pack after we finish dinner. It's the least I can do, since I'm the one breaking our deal."

Azure wanted to ask him about Vienna, wanted to know if they'd rekindled their romance, but wasn't brave enough to ask. "Have you met someone?" she asked, despite the painful lump in her throat. "Someone you're interested in being with?"

"Is that what you think? That I want to move someone else in here?"

"What do you expect me to think, Harper? We're supposed to play husband and wife for the next three months, but now you're calling the whole thing off after only two weeks."

"Because living with you is making me crazy!"

"But you just said I've been a model houseguest!" she shouted back. "Which one is it?"

"Damn it, Azure, don't you get it? Isn't it obvious?" Harper growled, ripping off his apron and throwing it down on the counter. "Do I need to spell it out for you?"

"Yeah, Harper, you do because I don't know what the hell you're talking about."

"I'm talking about wanting you, Azure! About wanting to kiss you and caress you and love you until I'm spent!"

Chapter 14

Unable to speak, Azure stared at Harper, wide-eyed and openmouthed. Convinced she looked like the visual definition of the word *gobsmacked,* she closed her dry, parted lips. *Did Harper just say what I* think *he said?* Azure shook the thought right out of her head. *No, no, no. I must have misheard him. Must get my hearing checked as soon as—*

"My attraction to you is destroying me, Azure. I can't concentrate at work, and most days I feel like I am functioning at a grade-two level…."

Azure stood rigid with shock. His confession blew her away. She had no idea Harper felt that way, and to her amazement, the more he spoke the more aroused she got.

"I fantasize about making love to you, about being buried deep inside you twenty-four-seven, and it's killing me."

Her heartbeat accelerated, raced faster than the engine in a European sports car. His words gave her a rush of pleasure, caused tingles to spark between her legs. She heard the frustration in Harper's voice, the angst, and wanted to put him out of his sexual misery, but before she could confess her true feelings, he dropped another bombshell.

"I'm a gentleman, not a saint, and if you stay I'm bound to cross the line, so please leave while I still have a semblance of dignity." He dropped his hands at his sides, his shoulders bent, a defeated expression on his face. "I'm sorry things didn't work out."

His gaze captured her, held her in its powerful grip. And when a sad smile touched the corners of his lips, Azure fell apart at the seams. She struggled to breathe, to think, to remain upright. Gathering herself as best she could, Azure waited until she was calm and composed before speaking. "Can I at least have dinner before you kick me out?"

Her joke fell flat, ratcheting up the tension another nerve-racking degree. Harper didn't laugh, he just stood there, bracing his hands against the island, staring at her with sad eyes. Seeing his vulnerability only made Azure want him more. She craved his kiss, his caress, but she knew Harper would push her away if she touched him. This was it. They were done. Over. And the smart thing to do now was to leave before she acted on her desires and shamed herself.

"I guess this is goodbye, then," Azure said in a voice she didn't recognize. It was thin, but harsh, and left an acerbic taste in her mouth. "I'm going to go pack."

He gave a solemn nod. "Just call down if you need anything."

"Don't worry about me. I'll be fine."

"Are you going to be okay? You seem—"

"Why do you care?" she snapped as she snatched her purse off the couch. "We're through."

As she turned toward the staircase, Harper seized her hand. Moving with more finesse than an action hero, he captured her around the waist and backed her up against the fridge.

Azure was trapped, with nowhere to go, and fighting mad. She struggled against him, tried valiantly to break free, but Harper clasped her wrists and pinned them to her sides.

"Let me go."

"Not until you calm down. You're in no shape to pack, let alone drive home."

"What home? I have nowhere to go," she snapped, glaring at him. "I rented my room to Maggie's boyfriend until January, remember?"

"I'll pay for you to stay at the St. Regis."

Azure rolled her eyes to the kitchen ceiling. "How noble of you."

An amused grin appeared on his face, and for a moment, Azure almost forgot why she was mad at him. His smile was gorgeous, so rich and luminous, it took her breath away. That's why she had to leave, why she had to get far away from him. Harper was right. They had a deal, and it would be foolish to change the terms now. It didn't matter that she craved him, didn't matter that her body was infected with lust. It was time to get the hell out of Harper's house. And not a moment too soon.

"You're wearing a new perfume."

Frowning, she slanted her head to the right. His words left her confused, bewildered. *Why is Harper doing this to me?* she wondered, fiddling with her pearl necklace. *Why is he prolonging my misery?*

"What's it called?"

"Love-struck."

"How fitting," he whispered, lowering his mouth, "because that's how I feel every time you walk into a room."

Azure felt his hands skim her breasts, and shivered when he flicked his thumb over a nipple. It was a high-voltage charge that fused her eyes to his lips, and her hands to his chest. "Stop," she croaked, hating that her order sounded more like a desperate plea. "I don't want this, and I don't want you, so—"

Harper crushed his lips to her mouth.

The kiss unleashed his desire, unleashed the pent-up emotions he'd been battling for the past two weeks. To his surprise, Azure kissed him back. Matched his heat, his urgency, gave herself willingly to him. He sucked on her bottom lip, teased and licked it with his tongue. Her mouth felt amazing, tasted sweet, too, but it didn't quench his body's thirst.

He needed more.

A *lot* more.

Aroused by the feel of her body, so close to him, he gave his hands license to roam down her arms, along her shoulders, to palm and fondle her breasts. His carnal desires seized him, demolished what little self-control he had left. Screw their deal, his promise. He'd just have to apologize later. After they finished making love in his bedroom. *If* they ever made it there.

The kiss sent Azure's body into another hemisphere. It was a passionate, openmouthed kiss, one that instantly put her in an erotic mood. She kissed him deeply, intensely, with total abandon. Relishing the moment, she savored the feel of his strong hands clutching her waist, keeping her in place, right where he wanted her. Harper glided his hands up, down, over and across her horny, inflamed body. His eagerness excited her, made her even hungrier for him.

Harper unzipped her dress, watched as the fitted black garment sailed to the floor. Mesmerized by the glorious shape of Azure's body, he stood there for a long moment, admiring every delicious slope and mouthwatering curve.

Feeling exposed, Azure raised her hands to cover her breasts.

"Don't." His tone was harsh, the word a fervent order. "I want to see you. All of you."

Slowly, he traced a finger over her collarbone, down the length of her arms and along the lace detail of her La Perla bra. Azure shivered. Her panties were drenched, soaking wet, and her legs were trembling. Azure loved what Harper was doing with his hands, loved how desirable he was making her feel. He whispered naughty words in her ear, squeezed her butt like a roll of Charmin, and vowed to give her a night of pleasure she'd never forget. Harper made good on his promise with every kiss, every caress, and when he ground his erection against her hips Azure moaned in his ear.

"You're gorgeous, Azure. So damn sexy I could come just looking at you."

Unhooking her bra, he sprayed kisses from her ears to her shoulders. Harper palmed her breasts, roughly tweaked each nipple. It was sweet torture. Pleasure to the ninth degree. Yanking down her thong panties, he slid his hand along her swollen lips, then dipped the tip of his finger inside her. "You're so wet. Wet for me, and only me. Right, baby?"

Azure nodded meekly. She was so aroused, so hot and bothered she didn't trust herself to speak for fear another desperate plea would tumble out. Harper plunged a finger inside her, and Azure all but lost her mind. Throwing her head back, she cried out. He probed her sweet spot, swirled and whirled his thumb as if it were an instrument of pleasure. Azure's moans drowned out the music, rose to a dizzying, high-pitched crescendo. They were just fooling around, enjoying each other's bodies, but Azure felt an intense spiritual and emotional connection to Harper. This wasn't about sex, wasn't about scratching an itch. Harper truly cared about her. It was evident in his kiss, his gaze, the gentle, loving tone of his voice. And the more he caressed her, the deeper she fell in love with him.

His fingers ignited an orgasm between her legs. Trembling from head to toe, she rocked her hips against his fingers.

Azure couldn't catch her breath. Her body was humming, throbbing something fierce. She was losing it. Had been ever since she'd walked into the Hamilton family estate and seen Harper standing beside the fireplace. From the moment Azure saw him, she'd wanted him. Wanted to act out every fantasy, every erotic dream she'd ever had about him. And tonight, she planned to enjoy the privileges and benefits of being Harper's lawfully wedded wife.

Crazed with desire, she pushed Harper's V-neck sweater up off his shoulders and tossed it down to the floor. It was time to return the favor. Time to give as good as she got. Parting her lips, she leaned in and sucked his nipple into her mouth. She darted her tongue over the bud, flicked and licked and sucked it as if it were a chocolate chip.

Cradling her to his chest, Harper released a loud, savage groan. Each slow, deliberate flick of Azure's tongue pushed him to the brink, to the point of no return. There was no turning back now, and Harper wasn't letting Azure go until he'd had his fill of her. Was that even possible? He could never get tired of this, of her. When he was with Azure, everything made sense, everything felt right. Tonight, her pleasure was his mission, his top priority, so he cupped her face and made love to her lips with his mouth.

The deep, wet kiss brought out the animal in Azure. She rocked against him, rotated her hips like a seasoned pole dancer.

Sensing it was time, Harper took off his jeans and boxer shorts.

Azure gasped. He was thick, longer than a ruler, and standing tall and erect—for her. She took his length in her hands, stroked it as if it were the finest work of art. Azure wanted to do naughty things, the kinds of things she saw in erotic French films, so she dropped to her knees to please her husband. Licking the tip of his erection made *her* hot down below.

Gripping his shaft, she lowered her head and took him in her mouth. Taking off her pearl necklace, Azure swathed it around his length like a choker, then rolled it up and down his erection, all the while showering his erection with soft kisses.

"That's it, baby, work those juicy, wet lips." Harper stirred himself inside her. Pleasure paralyzed his tongue, and all he could do was groan and grunt. It was their first time, but Azure knew how to use her mouth and lips and hands to please him.

Gripping her hips, he lifted her off the floor and set her down on the kitchen counter. Panting, she hooked a leg around his waist, drawing his sex closer to her. The fruit basket toppled over, utensils went flying and the water pitcher crashed to the floor. Water pooled at Harper's feet, but the ice-cold liquid didn't reduce his sweltering body temperature.

Still feasting on her mouth, he spread her legs wide open and stroked her slowly with the head of his shaft. He teased her with it, drew it along her sweet spot—slowly, slowly, back and forth. Crying out, Azure begged him to enter her.

Harper granted her wish.

In a blink, he was inside her, thrusting like a man possessed. And he was. It was a tight, snug fit, and when Azure squeezed her pelvic muscles, his eyes rolled to the back of his head.

Scared they were going to topple over, Azure gripped Harper's shoulders and inched over to the right, to the center of the counter. The move didn't slow him down. Harper was a beast. He took everything she gave and more. He drew his tongue over her earlobe, sucked her nipples and playfully grabbed fistfuls of her hair. And Azure loved every wicked minute of it. His grunts and groans were as intoxicating as the scent of their lovemaking, and the ecstasy of making love to Harper—the star of her teenage fantasies—made Azure want to weep. To shed big, fat, sloppy tears. Her feelings were that strong, that intense.

"Oh God, baby, you feel amazing," Harper rasped, kissing her hard on the lips.

Azure raked her fingernails through his hair, then dragged them down his back and gripped his butt, drawing him deeper inside her.

Harper increased his thrusts. He wanted to possess her, wanted to brand every inch of her flesh with his lips and tongue and hands. He'd never known a pleasure so sweet, never been with a woman whose touch made his entire body convulse.

Shudders zipped down Harper's spine. He groaned, cursed, babbled like the forty-year-old virgin of film the first time he got a taste. Azure was perfect for him in every way, and he'd give her the world or die trying, as long as she never, ever left his side. "I don't think I can last much longer," he confessed. "Sorry, baby, I'll make it up to you later. I promise."

"I'm going to hold you to that," she purred, nipping at his bottom lip.

Sweat dripped from his face, and fatigue clung to his limbs, but her kiss energized him, made him feel like the world's strongest man. Harper gazed down at Azure, and what he saw in her eyes made his heart stop. He didn't want to believe, but there was no doubt about it. Azure loved him—completely, fully, deeply. It was written on her face. He saw it in her smile, felt it in her touch, heard it when she screamed out his name.

"Hold on, baby, I'm right behind you. I'm coming… I'm coming…." Harper kissed her, cradled her tenderly in his arms when she started to quiver and shake. Loving her, moving and thrusting inside her was exhilarating, more dazzling than a million sunsets. Harper loved the way Azure cried out, loved how she lost complete and utter control as she came.

Fireworks exploded behind Azure's eyes. Her body shook, trembled from head to toe. She floated high off the ground, soared to a pleasure-filled world. Feeling as free as a hang glider floating in the sky, she closed her eyes and snuggled into her husband's chest. The last thing Azure remembered before drifting off to sleep was Harper picking her up, kissing her softly on the lips and carrying her out of the room.

Chapter 15

Yawning, Azure stretched her sore arms lazily in the air. She blinked and stared out into the pitch-black darkness. *Had it all been a wonderful dream?* she asked herself, rubbing the sleep from her eyes. *A sensual, erotic dream that had finally resulted in the big O? Not once, not twice, but three incredible times!*

Slowly, the living room came into focus. Sunlight trickled in from the sides of the blinds, showering the space with warmth and Azure could hear tree branches scraping against the windows. The air was saturated with the scent of coffee and cinnamon. Right on cue, her empty stomach growled like a wildebeest.

Azure glanced around, and when she saw the state of Harper's home her mouth fell open. The end table was on its side, magazines were strewn across the carpet and clothes littered the floor. As she assessed the damage, memories of last night flooded her mind. After making love in the kitchen, they'd stumbled into the living room and collapsed onto the sofa and fallen into a deep, comalike sleep. Azure knew she should get up and start getting ready for work, but she didn't have the strength to move. Not after that wild, raucous sex session with Harper. *I can't believe we actually had sex on the kitchen counter!*

Combing a hand through her tangled, tousled hair, she chastised herself for losing control. Azure couldn't blame her impetuous behavior on alcohol, because she hadn't had a drop, and there wasn't a full moon last night, so what had gotten into her? What had caused her to be so irresponsible? She'd never had unprotected sex before, but last night she'd done it twice. And even now, despite the risks, she was raring to go again. But this time she'd make sure they used a condom, and she'd stay in control. No screaming, no moaning, no cursing like a trucker—

"Good morning, baby. How did you sleep?"

Azure hopped like a cricket at the sound of Harper's voice. Yanking the blanket off the back off the couch, she pulled it up to her chin and used it to cover her naked body. "Ah, fine, thanks. You?"

"Great. I haven't felt this good since I whipped Jake in a game of one-on-one basketball!"

Chuckling, Harper strode into the living room, looking undeniably sexy in his black silk pajama bottoms. The sight of his broad, bare chest made Azure's pulse roar to life. He put the silver tray he was carrying on the glass table, and sat down beside her on the couch. "Hungry? I brought you hot chocolate, a raisin bagel and a bowl of fruit."

Sitting up against the cushions, she tucked the blanket under her arms and reached for one of the oversize mugs topped with whipped cream. The blanket slipped back down, but Azure caught it before it exposed her swollen, tender breasts.

"Azure, don't."

"Don't what?"

Harper cupped her chin, forced her to meet his gaze. "Don't hide from me, Azure. I love your body. You're perfect, baby, just the way you are."

"Have you been drinking?" she joked, laughing nervously. "You must be, because I'm the furthest thing from perfect."

"You're doing it again."

"Doing what?"

"Using sarcasm to avoid the truth."

Harper leaned into her, brought his body three inches closer and his mouth into kissing distance. The air was charged with desire, an excitement so electric, Azure could feel it.

"Do you regret making love to me?"

"No, never." A smile gripped her lips. "I loved every minute of it."

"Are you sure?"

"Positive. Do you?"

"Hell no!" Harper wore a devilish smirk, one she'd never seen spread across his face before. "Actually, I was hoping we could do it again. And again. *And* again."

"You don't even have to ask." To prove it, Azure pressed her chest against his and brushed her lips against his mouth. His lips were flavored with strawberries and tasted so sweet she licked them with her tongue. Azure felt the blanket slide down her chest and gather around her waist. Clutching it in her hands, she flung it to the floor and slid onto Harper's lap. She wanted to feel his hands—in her hair, on her breasts, buried between her legs—and didn't want any barriers between them. Not now, not ever.

"You have the sweetest lips. They're so moist and juicy," he praised, between kisses. "I know this wasn't part of our deal, but I can't go back to the way things were, Azure. I desire you too much."

Feeling light-headed and weak, like a thrill seeker staggering off a five-hundred-foot roller coaster, Azure closed her
eyes and waited for the room to stop spinning. Her mind went
blank, and her pulse pounded in her ears. Harper brushed her
hair away from her face, drew his fingertips through the thick,
tangled ends. His eyes spoke to her, revealed hidden feelings
and emotions. Azure didn't want to ruin the moment by bab-
bling, or stumbling over her words, so she pulled him down
on top of her and devoured his lips with her mouth. Harper
was her lawfully wedded husband—at least in the eyes of the
court—and Azure was enjoying every single perk that came
with being his wife.

"Lie back and spread your legs wide for me," he whispered,
showering her lips with hungry, urgent kisses. His fingers
found her nipples, then the slick, wet treasure between her
legs. "I want to taste you. Here."

Azure tensed, sat up to prevent him from replacing his
hands with his mouth. "No."

"You trust me, don't you?"

"That's not it… I've never, you know."

"Received oral sex? Why not?"

Staring down at her hands, she shrugged in response. "No
one's ever offered before."

"Well, I am," he told her. "I want to make you come over
and over *and* over again."

For the first time in her life she was speechless, struck
dumb by shock. Azure didn't know what to say. The thought
of Harper licking her sweet spot caused desire to singe her
flesh. According to her female colleagues, men never offered oral sex— and Azure knew if she told her cowork-
ers what Harper had said, they'd pass out. "I guess it's true
what they say after all," she teased. "Lawyers *do* have a way
with words."

"I'm not trying to sweet talk you, or run a game on you. I

care deeply about you, and it blows my mind that we're here, together, making love."

"Harper, that's crazy. You're a smart, successful attorney who can have any woman he wants, and I'm just a magazine reporter, who, according to my mom, needs a better body."

Harper cupped her chin and forced her gaze to meet his. "Azure, you're beautiful. Period. It doesn't matter if you're wearing a designer dress, a business suit or those tiny workout shorts I love so much." He winked, then leaned in and softly kissed her lips. "Baby, every time I see you, you leave me breathless. Every. Single. Time."

He kissed her again, and again, and again. They kissed and teased, fooled around like a pair of inebriated college kids making out on their parents' couch. Harper dipped a finger into his mug, scooped up some whipped cream and rubbed it over Azure's nipple. Then he covered her breast with his mouth—licking and slurping and sucking the sweet cream. His touch triggered an avalanche of pleasure in her body. Her breathing accelerated, the tips of her ears tingled and she trembled from head to toe. Harper carried kisses down the length of her body, then positioned himself between her legs.

"Harper, are you sure about this? This is all new to me."

"We'll go slow, and if you want me to stop, just say the word."

"Just say the word?" she repeated, a sly smile tickling her lips. "Is there a code word in *Sex for Dummies* that I need to know about or something?"

"You're such a smart-ass."

"I know, and you love it!"

"You're right, baby. I do." Harper cupped her butt. "And I love this, too."

Harper slid his hands down her hips, drew them across every curve and slope. He licked around her belly button, kissed it, caressed it, poked his tongue inside it. Every time

Azure thought he was going to replace his fingers with his mouth, he'd find another part of her body to tease, to torment, to infect with desire. The anticipation was killing her. It was too much. Enough to make her lose her mind, and the last bit of pride she had left. Begging was beneath her, something only male R&B singers did, but if Harper didn't put her out of her misery soon, that's exactly what she was going to do.

Harper blew a warm, light breath between her legs.

Once, twice, three mind-numbing times.

He parted her lips with his tongue, and when he slid the tip inside her, Azure shivered. Moaning her pleasure, she closed her eyes and hiked her leg up on the side of the couch. Wanting to be in control, she clutched his head to keep his talented tongue in place, and slid closer. He nursed on her core, slurped and sucked her juices as if he were drinking from the wellspring of life. Her body went haywire, quaking, trembling and vibrating. Harper's tongue rode her clitoris, and each urgent, tantalizing stroke brought Azure one step closer to ecstasy.

"You're without a doubt the sexiest, most erotic woman I've ever been with," he said, reaching up and roughly cupping her breasts. "I could never get enough of this, baby, could never get enough of tasting your sweet, juicy lips."

Talking dirty always drove Azure over the edge, and the raunchy, explicit things Harper was saying triggered the most explosive orgasm ever. That, and how eagerly he was lapping his tongue against her clitoris.

An earthquake erupted between Azure's legs.

She couldn't stop shaking, couldn't control the tremors that rocked her body.

Azure felt Harper on top of her, kissing her lips, stroking her hair, whispering soft, sweet words in her ears. Closing her eyes, she basked in the indescribable beauty of the moment. This was happiness, joy. Being with Harper—experiencing the full extent of his love—was the greatest feeling in the world. And for the first time ever she felt whole, worthy. Azure wanted to curl up in Harper's arms and go to sleep, but the desire to please him was overpowering.

"Baby, what are you doing?"

"Returning the favor," she purred, caressing his face while stroking his erection to life with the other hand. "Ready for another round?"

"Yeah, but take it easy on me this time. I'm playing basketball with the guys at noon, and if I show up limping Jake will kill me on the boards—"

"You're not going anywhere."

"I'm not?"

A slow, easy smirk claimed her lips. "Nope. You're sick."

"I am?"

"Yup, you have a twenty-four-hour bug, and it's pretty nasty," she told him, her tone matter-of-fact, "but don't worry. Your sexy wife is going to nurse you back to health."

"You are, huh?"

"I sure am, and once I'm finished with you, you'll feel as good as new."

Harper sat back with a flourish and clasped his fingers behind his head as if he were sunbathing on the beach. And the more he posed and profiled, the harder Azure laughed.

"Well, what are we waiting for, Nurse Does-A-Body-Good?" he joked, winking lasciviously at her. "Go ahead and *do* me!"

Chapter 16

*F*ive *more minutes and then we're out of here,* Azure decided, sneaking a look at her silver wristwatch bracelet. Her braised lamb sat on her plate, untouched, and her glass was full of a tasty mango drink, but she was itching to go home. *I've had about all I can stand of Eden, and if we don't leave soon, I'm going to blow.*

Dressed in Chanel from head to toe, Eden had breezed into the Schmooze Lounge smiling and waving at the patrons who gazed adoringly at her. After a quick hug to Azure, and kisses on Harper's cheeks, she'd sat down with a flourish and begun yapping about her crazy-busy modeling schedule.

"I can't believe you've never been to Cabo San Lucas, Alice." Making her hazel, oval-shaped eyes great big and wide, she gracefully ran a hand through her black, ridiculously long hair. "The island is to die for, and always crawling with A-list stars. You absolutely must stay at the Sea of Cortez Resort. It's breathtaking!"

Azure rolled her eyes. What was with the accent? Eden had been raised in Philly—like her—and the fake, haughty tone she'd adopted made her sound like a snob. At least to her. Harper seemed to be completely smitten with Eden, and the two of them had been laughing and joking all night. They were having such a good time Azure had started to wonder if Harper even remembered she was there.

"I was thinking of taking Azure to Cabo for the Christmas holidays," Harper said, putting his fork down on his empty plate. "Maybe you and your husband can join us. The more the merrier, right, Cupcake?"

A frown marred Eden's fine, delicate features. "I'll have to check with Renault and get back to you. Leonardo DiCaprio and his girlfriend are *very* close friends of ours, and they've invited us to go sailing in the Greek isles, which is absolutely one of my favorite things to do."

"Good for you," Azure grumbled, wishing she could cram a piece of garlic bread into her sister's big, boastful mouth.

"I'm hoping to make some headway with Leonardo, and on the blue, breathtaking seas is the perfect place to do it."

"Azure never mentioned you were an actress, as well." Harper picked up his glass and took a swig of his drink. "Is Leonardo helping you break into the business?"

"You could say that," she said coyly, batting her fake eyelashes at Harper. "My husband and I have an open marriage, and Leonardo is on the top of my sexual wish list!"

Harper choked on his martini. "Open, as in you date other people?"

"Among other things." Giggling, Eden flapped her thin, graceful hands in the air. "Don't look so stunned, you two. All the stars are doing it. Will and Jada, Sting and Trudy, Larry King and all of his ex-wives!"

Azure was too stunned to speak. And obviously Harper was, too. He was guzzling his drink as if it were holy water, and glancing over his shoulder as if he was scared Jesus himself was going to appear and strike them all dead.

"Who knows?" she uttered, coiling a lock of hair around her index finger. "Maybe one day you and my sister will be swingers, too."

"Hell no!"

Startled by the harsh bite in Harper's tone, Azure swung her head in his direction. His eyes were narrowed, it looked as if his jaw were wired shut and a scowl was clinging to his lips. He was breathing heavy, the way he did after they finished a vigorous round of lovemaking, and his face looked tense. Harper leaned over and draped an arm around her shoulders. Azure snuggled against him. Finally, he was showing her some affection, some attention, too.

Azure could stay in Harper's arms forever. His touch was addictive, and every moment of every day she found herself counting down the seconds until she'd see him again. It had been like that for the past three days, since the night he'd asked her to leave and all hell broke loose. Thinking about their first time—and their sumptuous morning after—made her body tingle. Azure had never been loved so fully, so deeply. No one had ever worshipped her with their lips, or given her one mind-blowing orgasm after another. Harper had taken the time to discover every single one of her hot spots and triggers and eagerly stroked every pleasure-filled zone.

For the past three days, they'd been playing and frolicking in bed, making love as if it were the first time for them both. And if not for Eden being in town, they'd be home, in bed, probably eating dessert off each other. Azure couldn't get enough of Harper, couldn't stand to be away from him, and when it came to Harper her body seemed to have a mind of its own. One kiss was all it took to make her wet. Two drenched her La Perla panties. Three turned her into a freak between the sheets who commanded the reins in the bedroom. Or the kitchen, or the staircase or wherever they were when the mood struck.

"Azure is the only woman I need."

Hearing Harper's sweet, heartfelt words, made Azure melt. Sighing inwardly, she nuzzled her face against his chin and wrapped an arm around his lean waist. *When we get home, I'm going to put it on him for real!*

"Oh, come on, Harper, everyone has a celebrity crush," Eden insisted. "There must be someone in the entertainment industry you'd like to spend the night with."

"You're right, there is," he conceded, wearing a rueful smile. "I'd love to have dinner with Judge Judy Sheindlin, but I just want to pick her brain, not see what's under her robe!"

Eden erupted in laughter, snorted so loud she attracted the attention of the other patrons dining in the lounge. Azure cracked up when she saw the stunned expressions on the faces of the reality TV stars seated nearby. It felt good being out, and although Azure had fun at all the social events Harper had taken her to over the past weeks, it was nice not having to pose for the cameras or play nicey-nice with all the stuck-up rich people in attendance.

"I'm sorry, ladies, but I've got to get going." Harper slipped on his leather jacket. "Drink and eat as much as you want. I'll settle the bill on my way out."

"Do you want me to come with you?" Azure asked, reaching for her purse. Two hours of Eden running her mouth was two hours too many, and when her sister wasn't flirting with Harper, she was yakking about her various modeling gigs or playing with her cell phone. Like right now. Her sister was so busy texting she didn't hear Harper say goodbye. "It's getting late, and after flying all day, I'm sure Eden's exhausted."

"Great idea, baby! I know my mom would love to see you...."

Yeah, dead, Azure thought, settling back into her seat. Her kid sister was obnoxious, but at least she wasn't plotting her demise. It was a case of the lesser of two evils, and Azure knew staying at the Schmooze Lounge with her sister was the safer, wiser choice. Azure hadn't seen Mrs. Hamilton since the wedding and had become a master at avoiding her angry, cynical mother-in-law. "On second thought, I think I'll stay. I don't know when I'll see Eden again, and we still have a lot of catching up to do."

"No problem." Standing, he grabbed the leather billet. "Call me when you're finished up here, and I'll come back and pick you up."

"Go on, Harper. I'll be fine."

Harper bent down and stole a kiss from her lips. Azure enjoyed the unexpected surprise, the flutter of excitement his touch caused, and hoped he did it again. And again.

"There are a bunch of thug wannabes in here tonight, and I don't want anyone hassling you while you're waiting outside at the cab stand. It's not safe, Azure. Anything can happen."

"Baby, I can handle myself." Smirking, she patted the front of her oversize designer purse. "I have pepper spray."

Harper didn't laugh, didn't even crack a smile. "I'm serious, Azure."

"So am I. If anyone gets too close, or starts any mess, I'm sprayin' their ass!" Azure cracked up, but when she saw Harper's face cloud with anger, her giggles dried up. Then she remembered. Remembered how Harper's ex had hooked up with a rapper at a trendy, upscale bar like this. Was that what Harper was worried about? That someone else would catch her eye and she'd go willingly to his bed? The thought was ludicrous, so outrageous Azure had to stop herself from laughing out loud. Harper was the only man for her, the only man she wanted to spend her days and nights with, and she would never do anything to break his trust. And later, when they were in bed, she was going to tell him just that. "I'll be home by ten," she promised, hoping to put him at ease, "and not a second later—"

"Just call."

Azure didn't know if it was the sharpness of his tone or the intensity of his gaze that made her girly parts tingle, but she wanted Harper right then and there. She imagined them going at it, shocking diners by getting down and dirty on their glass table.

At the thought, her conscience pelted her with guilt. She combed a hand through her hair and fanned her face with the other. Azure wondered if there was a patch or a gum or a support group—something, anything—that would stop her yearning, her desperate longing for Harper. Her desire for him was insatiable, spiraling out of control, and Azure feared if she didn't get a grip soon she was going to mess up the good thing they had going. "Okay, Harper, I'll call you in a couple hours. Happy now?"

"Immensely, but I'll show you my gratitude later. In the bedroom."

Azure bit her fingernail, thought about all the wicked things she was going to do to him in his plush, king-size bed. "I can hardly wait."

Another quick kiss—one that kindled her body's fire—and Harper was gone, stalking through the restaurant lounge with purpose, intent, as if he owned the joint. Azure watched him stroll through the waiting area and noticed all the hungry stares on the faces of the female patrons. *That's right, chicks, he's mine all mine and I've got the wedding ring to prove it!*

"Harper and Alice sitting in a tree, k-i-s-s-i-n-g," Eden sang, hopping around in her seat like the Energizer Bunny. "Girl, you're so hot for that man I bet your panties are soaked!"

Azure crossed her legs. She wished she could deny it, but it was true. She desired Harper, craved him, longed to be back in the comfort of his strong arms. His kiss ignited a firestorm within her, one that made her weak in the knees and hot all over, and it was hard remaining in her seat when everything in her wanted to chase him down.

"When Mom told me you got married, I thought she was kidding, but now that I've met Harper I understand your haste to jump the broom." Grunting, Eden licked her lips. "I'm not even attracted to black men, but Harper Hamilton has it seriously going on. If you weren't my sister, I'd be all over that man!"

"Thanks, I think."

"I want to know all the details, so dish. Where did you guys meet? How did he propose? And most importantly, when are you going to make me an auntie?"

Azure giggled. Pretending she didn't hear the last question, she briefly answered the first two. "Harper and I went to school together, and when I interviewed his family last month—"

"Hold that thought," Eden said, raising a finger in the air. She scooped her cell phone up off the table, tilted her head to the side and cooed a high-pitched greeting. "Renault, darling, did you finally seal the Victoria's Secret deal?"

Azure allowed her gaze to wander, and when it landed on a familiar face—a slim, brown-eyed guy with a serious, take-no-prisoners demeanor—she racked her brain to remember his name. Griffin…Griffin…Griffin Jackson! The soft-spoken attorney worked at the Hamilton family law firm, and although they'd only met once, Azure liked him. She wondered why he was sitting at the bar, alone, on a Friday night, but before she could even think of going over to greet him, Eden started wailing.

"What do you mean they changed their mind!" she yelled, gripping her cell phone. "This is *not* my fault! I did everything you asked me to. I lost weight, I had electrolysis treatments…"

Azure shivered. *That* sounded painful.

"Get me in that show, Renault! You're my manager. It's your job!" Her accent fell away. Her tone grew harsh, gruff. She was talking loud, spitting her words out faster than a rapper rocking the stage on 106 and Park. "Well, maybe if you spent more time booking me gigs, instead of boozing it up at the casino, my career wouldn't be going down the drain!"

Eden clicked off the phone and hurled it into her purse. Slumping back in her seat, as if she was trying to disappear in her leather, padded chair, she stared out into space.

"Is, um, everything okay?" Azure wanted to kick herself for asking such a dumb question, but she didn't know what else to say. "Do you want to talk about it?"

"Victoria's Secret doesn't want me," she croaked, her bottom lip trembling. "They dropped me from their Christmas fashion show."

"Don't worry, Eden. There will be lots of other jobs."

"But I wanted that one!"

Azure wore a sympathetic smile. "You'll get something bigger and better. You'll see."

Tears splashed onto her little black dress, and her nose started running like a leaky faucet. "Don't you get it? I'm finished. Done. My modeling career is over!"

"Eden, you're only twenty-seven."

"I might as well be eighty," she muttered, folding her arms. "Twenty-seven is ancient in the modeling world. The jobs are drying up, and these days no one wants to book me."

Azure tried to empathize, to comfort her younger sister, but it wasn't easy. All her life, Eden had teased and ridiculed her and even after all these years, her cruel taunts still played in her mind. "You're still young," she said, pulling her chair closer and rubbing Eden's back, "and there are a lot of other things you can do besides modeling."

"Like what?"

"Well, what do you like to do?"

"I—I—I don't know," she stammered, snatching a napkin off the table and cleaning her face. "I've never done anything besides modeling, and to be honest, I don't even know what I like."

"Then let's talk, and generate some ideas. How does that sound?"

"You make it sound so easy. I'm not like you, Alice. I'll never have the life you have."

"The life I have?" she repeated, confused. "What are you talking about?"

"You have the best of both worlds. You're smart *and* beautiful."

At her sister's words—words of admiration and respect—Azure's world flipped upside down on its head. *Did Eden just pay me a compliment? A real, genuine compliment?*

"All I have are my looks. That's it." Eden blew into her napkin. "I don't have a master's degree to fall back on, and because the modeling world is so cutthroat, I've made very few friends in the business. I don't have anyone, Alice. Don't you get it?"

"You'll always have me, Eden. We're sisters. I'll help you get through this."

"God, my life is such a mess! What am I going to do? I have nothing!"

"Don't talk like that. You have your home, your family and Renault."

Her sister gave a cold, bitter laugh. "Right. All that man cares about is himself."

"You guys will be okay. He supports you and loves you—"

"Not unconditionally. Not the way Harper loves you."

Azure gave a nervous laugh, shifted around as if she were sitting in the proverbial hot seat. She needed a minute, a moment to process her sister's words. Could it be true? Did Harper share her feelings? He was everything she wanted, needed and more. Attentive, loving, so damn tender she teared up just thinking about all the sweet things he'd said to her last night in bed.

"Alice, that man's crazy about you. I see it in the way he looks at you, the way he touches you. It's as if you are the only woman in the world. He's blind to every other girl, and it's obvious that he loves you very much." Eden made a face. "I've always been jealous of you, and after meeting Harper, I hate you even more!"

Azure was glad she was sitting down, because keeling over in her striped, fitted Michael Kors dress wouldn't have been cute. "Jealous of me?" she repeated, touching a hand to her pounding chest. "Why? I'm not thin, or glamorous, or—"

"You have everything going for you, that's why. A successful career, tons of friends, a ridiculously gorgeous man who only has eyes for you. I'd trade places with you in a heartbeat!"

To make her sister laugh, she teased, "But then you couldn't have Leonardo DiCaprio."

"*But* I'd have Harper Hamilton." A devilish twinkle in her eyes, she seductively licked her lips. "Sounds like a fair trade to me. Your new husband is filthy, stinkin' rich *and* fine as hell!"

Chapter 17

"*Y*ou've been a naughty boy, and Madame Adore is going to make you pay!"

Harper glanced up from his computer. His beer bottle slipped from his hand and fell to the carpet. Bolting upright in his chair, he watched with wide eyes and a dry mouth as Azure sashayed into his office wearing a tight, see-through french maid costume that kissed every glorious curve on her body. She was clutching a leather whip and smacked it on the floor as she strutted toward him. "Azure, baby, what's, um, going on?"

"It's Madame Adore," she reminded, wearing a saucy smile. "Now stand up."

Harper shot to his feet. He'd never been so turned on, and when Azure came around the desk and pushed him up against the wall, he felt an electric shock rip through him. He opened his mouth, but she silenced him by pressing a finger to his lips.

"No talking." Azure gave his belt buckle a hard tug, then unzipped his jeans. *"Relax, baby, and let Madame Adore make all your fantasies come true."*

Then she lowered herself to the carpet, yanked down his boxer briefs and sucked his erection into her warm, moist mouth—

"Earth to Mr. Hamilton."

Harper blinked twice, hit Pause on the erotic movie playing in slow motion in his mind and surged to his feet. Leveling a hand over his suit jacket, he cleared his throat and smiled apologetically at Judge Hackett. "I'm sorry, Your Honor, but can you repeat the question?"

"I know you're in baby-making mode," the judge began, her eyebrows raised sky-high, "and probably counting down the seconds until you see your blushing bride again, but while you're in court, please *try* and stay focused."

The court reporter tittered, the security guards posted on either side of the bench grinned and opposing counsel—a dark-skinned man who swaggered around like John Shaft—taunted him under his breath. Harper heard snickering in the gallery and knew Judge Hackett's dig would make it around the courthouse within the hour. He'd never had a problem with the wisecracking judge before, but if he wanted to remain on her good side and avoid being the butt of her jokes for the rest of the day, he had to get his head in the game.

Harper wore a confident smile, one to assure the judge that he was back in control, but inside he released a deep, troubled sigh. Courtrooms were his domain, his space, the place where he felt most comfortable, but these days, he'd rather be at home with Azure than in court. Thoughts of her consumed him, made it impossible for him to concentrate. His desire for her was destroying him. At the office, he fantasized about sexing her on the photocopier; in court, he imagined doing Azure on the judge's bench, and his lustful images were so intense he had to take a cold shower as soon as he got home. They didn't help any. Every time he showered, he wished Azure was with him, treating him to some of her amazing tongue action.

"Where is your client, Mr. Hamilton? It's nine o'clock, and I am prepared to start."

Harper scanned the gallery for Mr. Cheung. He didn't see the executive director of Stantec Engineering, but he did see his dad, Jake and Benjamin seated in the last row. Great, his family was there to witness his humiliation. Harper wanted to kick himself—hard. He couldn't believe he'd been so busy daydreaming about Azure he'd failed to notice that his client hadn't showed up. Worse still, he couldn't wipe her image out of his mind. Or the scent of her perfume. Or the sound of her voice when she came—

"I'm waiting, Mr. Hamilton. Where is he?"

"I don't know, Your Honor."

"Have you tried calling him?"

Dodging the question, he wore a confused face. "I spoke to Mr. Cheung this morning and he assured me he'd be here," Harper explained, hoping Judge Hackett wouldn't press him for more details because he didn't have any. He'd called the disgraced businessman at home, from his office, but when Azure came into the room to kiss him goodbye, he'd rushed his client off the phone and promised to phone him back. But Harper never did. One thing led to another, *and* another, and by the time they were finished making love he had to leave for court. In the car, he'd called Azure, and they talked until he reached the courthouse. Hence the reason why he looked like Boo-Boo the Fool now.

"This is very unlike Mr. Cheung. My client is a reliable, upstanding man, and he was looking forward to coming to court today and telling his side of the story."

"Then where is he, Mr. Hamilton?"

"I know this case has been delayed twice," he began, stepping forward, "but I'm requesting the case be remanded until next week."

Judge Hackett pointed a finger at him. "You have until one o'clock this afternoon, Mr. Hamilton, and not a second more. I suggest you go find your client *fast*."

"Thank you, Judge Hackett."

"And, Mr. Hamilton?"

"Yes, Your Honor?"

Her eyes were narrowed, but a smirk was playing on her thin pink lips. "No more daydreaming in court. Fantasize about your wife on your own time, got it?"

Snickers and chuckles swept through the courtroom.

The judge banged her gavel, and the crowd dispersed. Harper gathered his files, shoved them into his briefcase and sped out of the courtroom like a man on a mission.

"Son, a word."

Harper stopped and pivoted around. Luckily, it was just his father standing in the hallway, and not his cousin Jake or his brother Benjamin. "Hey, Dad, what are you doing here? I thought you were meeting one of your old law school buddies for breakfast."

"He canceled, so I came down here to watch the proceedings."

"Yeah, well, I'm sorry you wasted your time. My client didn't show, so I'm off to go find him and bring him to court before Judge Hackett issues a warrant for his arrest."

"I know, son. I saw, and I heard." Frank clapped him on the shoulder. "Come by the house for dinner tonight. Seven o'clock sharp."

Harper tried to remain calm, unfazed, but he was sweating like Mark Fuhrman on the witness stand. The last time his dad had summoned him to the house he'd dropped a bombshell. That was the miserable day he'd learned that his cousin

Jake was joining the family law firm. His life had never been the same again. Jake was a "man's man," one with killer charm and an eye for the ladies, and within weeks of joining the firm, he had not one, but two millionaire clients. "I can't, Dad." Harper shook his head to emphasize his point. "I need to prep for this case, and—"

"It's not a suggestion, son. It's an order."

Then Mr. Hamilton strode off.

When Harper turned into his parents' cobblestone driveway and saw all the sports cars parked along the circular lawn, he frowned. What were his brothers and cousins doing here? This afternoon, at the courthouse, he'd sensed that his father wanted to speak to him alone, in private, and Harper was curious how his family members factored into the equation.

Harper scooped his cell phone out of the center console and was surprised to see he had three new text messages from Azure. When he read the first one, a smile crowned his lips. The second message caused desire to shoot through his veins, and after reading the third text, he actually considered firing the engine back up and going home. *Seduction via BlackBerry,* he thought, sliding out of the car and heading up the walkway. *I like.*

His parents' longtime housekeeper let him in, and Harper headed straight for the media room. He could hear the TV and loud voices, and the scent of popcorn and beer saturated the air. As Harper entered the room and unzipped his jacket, he decided this was going to be a short, in-and-out visit. He wanted to get home—to Azure—and hoped when he did, she'd do everything she promised in her salacious text messages.

The Lakers game was on, trash talk was flowing and oversize food platters covered the bar. The whole gang was there, even Griffin, and the firm's toughest attorney rarely hung out after hours. At the end of a long workday, the Philly native would rather head home or to the gym, but Harper knew his colleague loved Southern food, and his dad had ordered enough catfish and black-eyed peas to feed the Philadelphia Eagles football team.

"We didn't expect to see you tonight, big guy," Benjamin said, acknowledging his older brother with a nod. "Did the little misses say it was okay for you to come watch the game, or did you have to sneak out of the house?"

Everyone in the media room chuckled.

"Go on, son. Fix yourself a plate."

Harper told himself he was just going to sample the honey barbecue wings, but after plucking one out of the container and taking a bite, he piled his plate high.

"What happened this afternoon in court?" Jake asked, glancing away from the TV. "Were you able to track down your client?"

Harper nodded. "I sure did, and Mr. Cheung was so convincing on the witness stand I saw a couple of the female jurors tear up when he talked about how the false accusations against him have affected his wife and children."

"I'm glad you redeemed yourself, cousin, because Judge Hackett is one of the toughest judges in the state, and if you piss her off you're toast!"

Chuckling, his dad clapped a hand on his shoulder and steered him toward the back of the room. "Harper, what can I get you from the bar?"

A picture of Azure, in his living room, sprawled out on his granite bar, her naked body glistening with sweat, flashed in Harper's mind. A shudder ripped down his spine, and his knees buckled like a folding chair. To keep from losing his footing and falling flat on his face, he gripped the counter. Images of a naked Azure had been popping up in his mind all day. All week actually. And it happened at the most inopportune times. Like when he was visiting a sick client in the hospital, in the middle of his talk at Temple's law school and every time he closed his eyes to pray for strength to overcome his overwhelming desire for her.

Harper tried to break free of his thoughts, but he couldn't get Azure out of his mind. She was his obsession. Had been since the first time they kissed. Making love to her, moving and thrusting deep inside her, was the greatest feeling in the world, but consummating their marriage had created a whole slew of new problems. Harper thought scratching the itch would make his desire for Azure go away, but these days he wanted her more than ever. She tasted just that sweet. Being with Azure was easy, effortless, as natural as breathing, and when they were apart, all he could think about was holding her again. Last night, after making love, they'd cuddled in bed for hours, talking about any and every subject—pop culture, their wedding ceremony, their dreams for the future. And for those few precious minutes before they drifted off to sleep, life was perfect. They were just a man and a woman without emotional baggage or painful pasts, a husband and wife team in every sense of the word.

"It's not a life-changing decision, son. Either you want a drink or you don't."

Harper blinked, returned his wayward mind to the present. "I'll have water," he croaked, loosening his tie. "A tall, cold glass of water."

His dad stepped behind the bar, and Harper slid onto one of the swivel stools. His parents' house resembled a show home, like something a Realtor would show to his celebrity clients, and as Harper glanced around the sleek, sophisticated media room, he couldn't help wondering if his dad kept buying expensive, state-of-the-art gadgets to fill the void in his life. His mother's career had taken off, and these days she spent more time at her downtown studio than at home. His father never complained, but Harper knew his dad didn't like his mom working eighty hours a week. Frank was old-fashioned, a traditionalist, who believed a woman's place was at home, with her family, not in the boardroom. Or in his mother's case, in glitzy European fashion houses.

"Everything okay at home?" Frank set a glass of water down in front of his son, then studied him closely. "Have you and Azure been getting along?"

In ways and positions you wouldn't believe. Harper grabbed his glass and didn't stop drinking until it was empty. "Yeah, Dad, things are going great," he said, resting his glass on the counter. "Azure's an amazing woman, and we have a real good time together."

...Kissing, sexing, doing things in the bedroom that are too hot for the adult-only channel! And as soon as I get home, I am going to do Azure in my Jacuzzi tub!

"Keep your wits about you, son. I don't want to get bamboozled like the last time."

Harper felt his jaw stiffen, his shoulders tense up. His dad's words bothered him, made him want to lash out. Azure was nothing like his ex, and he resented his father for implying that she was. Azure did everything right. She made a "perfect" cup of coffee, was a whiz at crossword puzzles, had a wicked sense of humor *and* kept him guessing in the bedroom. One day, she'd bum-rush him in the shower, the next she'd don a sexy costume and order him to bed and last night she'd pleasured him while he sat behind his desk reviewing his weekly agenda. What man wouldn't love that? "Azure is the best thing that ever happened to me, Dad. She's honest, and sincere, and I couldn't imagine my life without her."

Harper was surprised by the words that came out of his mouth, but they were true. And that scared him. His pulse took a nosedive and sweat skidded down the back of his pin-striped dress shirt. People in his social circle married for money or power, sometimes both, but rarely for love. The truth was, Harper didn't know if he believed in love, didn't know if he could ever fully trust anyone with his heart. Sure, his parents had been married for over thirty years, but these days they seemed distant and were often cold to each other.

"Azure seems like a nice young lady with a good head on her shoulders, but she's a reporter, and you know what they're like."

"No, Dad, I don't. Why don't you tell me?"

"Reporters are sneaky, cutthroat types who'll do anything for a headline. And," he stressed, raising a finger in the air, "your wife works for Leland Watson. That man would sell out his own mama for a story!"

"Dad, don't worry about me. Azure and I are good. She's got my back. I know it."

"I wasn't going to say anything, but after I watched you drown in court this morning…"

Hanging his head in shame, Harper pushed his gold-rimmed fork aimlessly around his plate. He waited for his dad to blast him for embarrassing the firm today in Judge Hackett's courtroom, but the rebuke never came. For the first time ever, his old man seemed more interested in his personal life than his career.

"I have nothing against your wife, son…."

A grin warmed his lips. *My wife.* God, he loved the sound of that. And the woman who filled his days and nights with joy. It was true. He loved her, loved living with her and making her smile. Azure always said exactly what was on her mind, and Harper liked knowing where he stood with her. She didn't play games or keep secrets from him, and after being engaged to someone who willfully misled him for months, he found Azure's candor refreshing. No way she'd ever play him. Not a chance. He didn't care what his dad or anyone else thought.

"To be honest, I'm more worried about Azure's boss screwing us over than I am about her," Frank confessed, stroking a hand over his jaw. "Leland Watson is as slimy as they come."

"Yeah, Dad, I know. Azure told me."

"Leland's had it out for me ever since I sued him, and I'm worried he's going to take his vendetta against me out on you or one of your brothers. I didn't want to do that interview last month, but your uncle Jacob insisted, so for the sake of peace, I went along with it."

Harper lowered his fork. "You sued Leland? What for?"

"It was a long, long time ago. I was fresh out of law school, and he was senior editor of a now defunct trashy gossip tabloid called *The Scoop*," Frank explained.

"Are you the reason the magazine folded?"

Frank gave a slow nod. Harper expected his dad to grin, to wear his proud trademark smile, but he didn't. His expression was somber and he was standing perfectly still, like one of the uniformed guards standing outside Buckingham Palace. "The magazine ran a fallacious story about one of my celebrity clients, so I smacked them with a million-dollar lawsuit. They eventually settled out of court, but the bad press ruined them, and they eventually closed up shop. Leland's been gunning for me ever since."

The room exploded in cheers.

"That was sick!" Benjamin shouted, jumping to his feet. "Dad, did you see that? Kobe rebounded his shot and dunked it in the defender's face!"

Frank turned toward the seventy-inch flat-screen TV just in time to see the replay. "I told you Kobe still had it! My boy's taking them all the way this year!"

"No way," Shawn said, shaking his head, "and the Chicago Bulls are definitely going to win this game."

Jake leaned forward in his seat. "Want to put your money where your mouth is?"

"You're on. A hundred bucks says that my team wins."

"A hundred bucks?" Jake flapped his hands in the air, as if he were fending off a colony of bees. "That's chump change. Don't talk to me until you're ready to make a grown-man wager. I'm talking five bills or more."

Harper blocked out the insults flying around the room. He had better things to do than listen to his brothers and cousins argue about who the best player was in the NBA. As he sat at the bar, eating his food, he gave more thought to what his father said. Harper knew his dad was only looking out for him, but he didn't like him bad-mouthing Azure. Her boss might be a shady double crosser, but she wasn't. They'd only been married for three weeks, but Harper felt as though he'd known Azure for years. And whenever she was interviewed, she always made him look like "the man." She gushed about his cooking skills, praised him for being a thoughtful, romantic husband and spoke with admiration about his family's charity, The Tuck Me In Foundation.

Feeling his cell phone vibrate, he pulled it out of his pocket. When he read the latest text message from Azure, he dropped his fork, grabbed his coat and headed for the door.

"Hey, where are you going?" Jake called out, peeling his gaze away from the television screen. "You just got here!"

Harper dashed across the room as if a pit bull were hot on his heels. "Gotta go, guys. The wife just paged me 911, and if I don't hurry, she'll start without me."

Chapter 18

Azure stared at the computer screen. Her fingers were poised to type, and the sunshine flowing through the open window made her office feel warm and cozy. Azure had everything she needed to create magic, to write an article that would knock her editor's socks off, but her mind was blank, as empty as a Hooters waitress with a seventy IQ.

Azure blocked out all the noises swirling around the office. This had never happened before. Usually, she sat behind her desk and the ideas flowed, but today she couldn't think of a single thing to write. *I wonder if staying up late has anything to do with it,* Azure thought, feeling a smile coming on. *I think all that wine-flavored body paint I licked off Harper's chest last night is messing with my concentration!*

To refocus her thoughts, Azure opened the draft she'd written last week but deemed too erotic to print. She reread it, ensuring that her ideas were complete and well expressed. It was no easy task, considering that the article had been inspired by Harper. Her editor would never publish *How to Unleash Your Inner Freak,* but writing it had been great fun, more enjoyable than watching a *Girlfriends* marathon on BET. Or in her case, an hour in bed with the man she loved.

Her office phone rang, and Azure snatched it up on the second ring. "*Eminence* magazine, Azure Ellison-Hamilton speaking."

"Is this my sexy, gorgeous wife?"

Azure felt a rush of divine pleasure at just the sound of Harper's rich, dreamy voice. They had been married for three blissful weeks, and had been spending all their free time together, but talking to him on the phone still gave her butterflies. Turning away from the computer screen, she sat back comfortably in her chair and twirled the phone cord around her index finger. "I was just thinking about you. How's your day going?"

"It got better the second I heard your voice."

A smile kissed her lips as she crossed her legs.

"Can you talk, or is this a bad time?"

Azure made a face but tried to keep the negativity out of her tone. "Unfortunately, I have all the time in the world. I have writer's block like you wouldn't believe."

"Maybe going dancing tonight at the 90 Degrees Nightclub with your dashing, new husband will get your creative juices going."

That, among other things. A laugh tickled Azure's throat and bubbled up out of her lips. To stifle her giggles, she deleted the salacious thought from her mind.

"So, are we on?"

"Baby, you don't even have to ask. You know I can never say no to you."

"Keep talking like that and I'll have to come down there and thank you in person."

"You better not. Our beauty editor hasn't forgiven me for

marrying you, her longtime crush, and if she sees us together she'll kick my butt for sure!"

"Don't worry, baby. I'll protect you."

"I love the sound of that." *And I love you, too* went unsaid. It wasn't time. They were lovers, and although Azure was starting to think they could make their marriage work for real, she wasn't going to ruin things by making any weepy declarations. Azure loved living with Harper, loved being his wife, and the thought of spending the rest of her life with him made her feel like crying tears of joy. For the first time ever, she was completely and truly happy, and she owed it all to Harper. He'd redefined her definition of love and made her realize she was worthy and enough, just as she was. It didn't matter what her mom or anyone else said. Love handles and cellulite be damned! She was a smart, vivacious woman who had everything going for her, and as long as she had Harper's love, she'd never want for anything.

"Common's album release party is tonight, and I want to go and show you off," Harper said, his voice taking on a cool, sexy edge.

"I'd love to go!"

"Wow, I'm surprised. I thought I'd have to bribe you with sexual favors."

"Not this time. I'm giving you the night off!" Azure giggled. "I heard on the radio that Demetri Morretti is in town, and I bet he'll be at Common's album release party. His publicist has been giving me the runaround for weeks, so tonight, I'm going to introduce myself and see if I can persuade him to give me an exclusive."

"Demetri Morretti's a bad boy who loves chasing after the ladies, and from what I've read he's a real handful."

"I'm not surprised. He *is* the highest-paid athlete in baseball."

Harper scoffed. "And that makes bedding everything in a skirt okay?"

"No, of course not. I never said it did."

Silence polluted the line. It stretched on for so long, Harper knew Azure had taken offense at what he said. He couldn't tell her the truth, not without looking insecure. "I hope he agrees to do the interview," Harper said through clenched teeth.

It was a lie. He didn't. Demetri Morretti, the hotshot major league baseball player with the golden arm and chiseled looks, made women all around the world squeal and swoon. What if Azure interviewed him and he made a move on her? Harper swallowed hard. It wasn't a question of "if it happened," but "when it happened." Five minutes alone with Azure, and Demetri Morretti would be smitten. That's what had happened to him. And every day Harper spent with her, his feelings grew deeper, stronger. To the point where just the thought of her spending time with another man made him break out in a cold sweat. Harper wasn't the jealous type, and he trusted her wholeheartedly, but that didn't mean he wasn't worried. He was. A lot.

"Do you have a problem with me interviewing Demetri Morretti?"

"Of course not. I support everything you do. You know that."

"I'm just checking," she said, her voice a stroke lower, softer, "because if you didn't want me to do it, I wouldn't."

"Really?"

"Harper, why does that surprise you? I'd never want to do anything to upset you, and if you weren't on board, I'd scrap the whole thing."

At her words, the tension in the air lifted and his anxiety disappeared. He couldn't wipe the goofy, lopsided grin off his face, and made a mental note to stop at Tiffany's on his way home. His wife deserved something extra special, and

Harper knew just what to get her. Something she could wear tonight to bed. Envisioning Azure naked, in nothing but the diamond necklace, made his heart race. "Are you sure you don't want me to swing by your office? We could have lunch, *then* each other."

"Goodbye, Harper," she sang, giggling. "I'll see you later."

"I can hardly wait…"

Smiling from ear to ear, Azure hung up the phone and turned back to her computer. No more distractions. She was going to sit in her chair, write the best damn article she'd ever written and then go home to her husband.

Pride and joy bubbled up inside her. *My husband.* If someone had told her that one day she would be Mrs. Harper Hamilton and live in one of the best neighborhoods in the city, she would have dropped them off at the state psychiatry center. Life had a funny way of working out, and Azure knew if she continued to make Harper happy inside and outside the bedroom, there'd be a chocolate-brown bundle of joy in their future—

Her phone rang, interrupting her thoughts. Azure knew it was Harper, calling back to flirt some more, and snatched up the phone. "Baby," she began, trying to sound stern but failing miserably, "if you keep calling me, I'll never finish this article and it's due tomorrow."

The line was quiet.

"Hello? Hello?"

"The Hamiltons are not the big, happy family they appear to be."

Frowning, Azure stared down at the phone receiver. This was the second crank call she'd received today, but this time the female caller wasn't whispering. Her voice was louder, stronger, dripping with malice and contempt.

"I know for a fact," the caller continued, "that Frank Hamilton has not always been faithful to his wife, and the evidence of his infidelity is out in the open for the whole world to see."

"Who is this?"

"I have proof to back up everything I've said."

Azure gripped the receiver, sat up straighter. "Who is this, and what do you want?"

Click.

Stunned, Azure listened to the dial tone pulse loudly in her ear. Hanging up the phone, she considered what the caller had said. Could Frank really be a cheater? And what "evidence" was the woman referring to? Widely known and respected around town, Frank Hamilton moved effortlessly around people of all socioeconomic backgrounds and races. There was even talk of him running for mayor in next year's election. With Frank's bigger-than-life personality he was a shoo-in to win, but a tawdry sex scandal would knock him clear out of the race.

Azure tapped her fingernails absently on her desk. A few weeks ago, she would have jumped all over this story—this was the kind of "dirt" her boss was hungry for—but now that she was in love with Harper, she couldn't stomach exposing his family's secrets.

Leaping out of her chair, she hustled through her office and out the open door. Bridgett Dalton, the gregarious beauty editor who never stopped running her mouth, would be able to tell her everything she needed to know about Frank Hamilton. And when Azure entered Bridgett's small, cramped office and found her sitting behind her desk trolling online gossip sites, Azure knew she'd come to the right place.

Chapter 19

The house was in darkness, but Azure heard music playing and wondered if Harper was cooking dinner again tonight. At the end of a long day, Azure loved nothing more than coming home, and as she unlocked the door and stepped inside the grand foyer a warm, peaceful feeling came over her. The lavish, two-story home was decorated with browns and creams, striking stone details and oversize bay windows that offered a breathtaking view of the vast, rolling landscape.

Emerging from his hiding place behind the door, Harper captured Azure around the waist. "I was just about to send out a search party for you!" he joked, wrapping her up in his arms and playfully nibbling her neck. "I thought you'd never get home."

Azure giggled when Harper flicked his tongue over her ear. "It's only five o'clock, Harper. Common's release party doesn't start for several hours."

"But I need you now, baby. I've been thinking about you all day."

"Awwwww." She sighed. "I missed you, too, baby."

"I have everything waiting in the bedroom. Wine, fresh fruit, whipped cream…"

"Wow, you thought of everything."

"All I need is you."

Turning her face toward him, she kissed him softly on the lips. "I want you, too, baby, but can we swing by the kitchen first? I really need a glass of cold water."

Harper released her, but not before giving her butt a hard squeeze. Inside the kitchen, he opened the cupboard, took out a glass and strode over to the stainless-steel fridge.

"How was your day?" Azure asked, unzipping her jacket and removing her scarf.

"Insane." Harper filled the glass with ice, then water. "My dad's in a bad mood, and this morning he ripped my head off for being five minutes late to the staff meeting. Normally, I'd shrug it off, but the whole team was there, and he tried to make me look stupid."

"I'm sure your dad didn't mean anything by it. He's probably just having a bad day."

"More like a bad *week*. He's been uptight and crabby since Monday."

Azure wondered if the female caller who'd phoned her this afternoon was threatening Frank. Or worse, blackmailing him. "Are you parents having problems in their marriage?"

Harper put the glass on the counter. "Not that I know of. Why?"

For hours after leaving Bridgett's office, Azure had sat at her desk, thinking about their hour-long conversation. Most of it was hearsay, and although Bridgett had no hard proof, she knew a lot about the Hamilton family. According to her colleague, rumors had existed for years that Frank Hamilton had indulged in a long-term affair that had resulted in a love child. Azure didn't know if Harper had ever heard the rumors, and wasn't brave enough to ask. He'd think she was being nosy, prying just for the sake of it, and Azure didn't want to ruin the great thing they had going. *But if the rumors ever became public...*

Shuddering at the thought, Azure swiped the water glass off the counter and took a long, thirst-quenching sip. Azure couldn't—no, wouldn't—let anyone ruin the Hamilton family. She had to protect her husband no matter the cost. A sex scandal would not only devastate Harper, but it would bring shame to the entire family and ruin their renowned law firm.

"I got an anonymous call this afternoon," Azure began, wiping her sweaty palms on the side of her belted sweater dress. She told Harper what the caller said, and when she was finished talking, she felt like a weight had been lifted off her shoulders. "I wasn't going to say anything, but I don't want there to be any secrets between us—"

"None of it's true," Harper snapped, cutting her off. "They're filthy lies that have been circulating for years, and were likely started by someone who has it out for my family."

"So you've heard the rumors before?"

"They've been around for as long as I can remember." Harper folded his arms across his chest. "My dad would never cheat on my mom. They love each other."

Azure held out her hands in a gesture of peace. She heard her cell phone ring in her coat pocket, but made no moves to answer it. There was nothing more important to her than being there for Harper, and she could tell by his stiff posture and cold, harsh tone that he was upset. "Baby, don't get mad at me. I was just asking. I told you about the call so we could figure out what to do together, as a team."

"I can't believe you fell for her lies! It's petty gossip. That's it. We're not doing anything about it, and as far as I'm concerned this conversation is over."

"Harper, I never said I believed her. I said she sounded convincing, that's all."

"Who is *she?*" he spat, pressing his palms down on the counter.

"I don't know. She wouldn't tell me her name."

"Did you even ask? Or try to find out what her story is?"

A cold chill crawled down Azure's spine. "I—I tried, but when I pressed her for more information, she hung up."

"Sure she did."

"I'm telling you the truth, Harper. I have no reason to lie."

"You've been lying since the day we met, *Alice.*" His eyes sliced across her face with the precision of a blade, and his cold, mirthless laugh pierced her ears. "Wow, you must really want to score some points with your boss. I know he's been pressuring you to dig up dirt on my family, but I never imagined you'd sink this low."

"Is that what you think? That I'm going to use this information against you and your family? I haven't told Leland about this, and I'm not going to."

"Right, I bet you've been shopping this story around for weeks."

Azure stood beside the pantry door, dead silent. Harper's ice-cold tone chilled her to the bone. Her body was numb with fear, and it felt as if her tongue was glued to the top of her mouth. This was her worst nightmare come true. Harper was mad at her, blaming her for something she didn't do, and his accusations hurt her deeply.

Hearing her cell phone start up again, Azure reached into her pocket. Taking the call would give Harper a moment to cool off, to consider what she'd said. The screen read Unknown Caller. Hoping it was Demetri Morretti's Chicago-based publicist, Azure put her cell to her ear and greeted the caller warmly. It was a challenge, and although she had a smile on her lips, her face felt harder than stone. "Hello, Azure Ellison-Hamilton of *Eminence* magazine."

"Frank Hamilton had an affair that resulted in the birth of a child. A daughter."

Azure gulped. *How did she get my cell phone number?* Her hands were shaking so hard, so slick with sweat the phone started to slip from her grasp. Catching it before it hit the floor, she swallowed the knot in her throat and prayed she wouldn't get sick on the marble floor.

Harper rubbed a hand over the back of his neck. His head was spinning like a yo-yo and it felt as if his heart were going to explode out of his chest. He had to get out of the kitchen, had to get away from Azure before he lost his temper. He started for the staircase, but when he heard the fear in her voice, he pivoted back around. Harper watched her eyes widened and the color drain from her pretty, delicate face.

"I'm not interested in the information," she said to the person on the line. "Please don't call me again. If you do, I'll contact the police and have you charged with…"

Harper held his breath. It was her anonymous source, the woman who'd called her earlier in the day. Had to be. Deep down, in his heart of hearts, he didn't believe that Azure would sell him out for a headline. The evidence against her was trivial, circumstantial at best, but Harper couldn't risk being humiliated again. His head and heart were in turmoil, both throbbing so hard, and so loud, he couldn't think straight. *What if he was wrong? What if it turned out that Azure and the caller were in cahoots? Would he be able to survive being burned by love again?*

"I don't believe you. You're lying!" Azure dropped the phone on the island, as if it were contaminated with a deadly virus, and stepped back. Shivering, she wrapped her arms around her shoulders and stared suspiciously at her discarded cell phone.

"Was that your anonymous source?"

Nodding, she dropped her gaze to the floor.

"What did she say?" Harper demanded, raising his voice.

"It doesn't matter. I'm not going to risk our relationship over a stupid story."

"Our relationship? What relationship? This was a business deal, and nothing more."

Azure swallowed. It took all of her effort to breathe, to keep from bursting into tears and falling to her knees. "I don't mean anything to you?"

Harper pretended not to hear the question. "I'm going to ask you one more time. What did your anonymous source say about my father?"

Raising her head, she faced him. His gaze was filled with hostility and aimed directly at her. Azure was prepared to fight, to defend her good name. She had to. Being without Harper was a terrifying concept, one she didn't think her heart could survive. "It's only going to hurt you and I won't do that."

"Tell me what she said, or else."

"Harper, calm down. Please, let me explain—"

"Explain what? How you stabbed me in the back to advance your career? I should have known you couldn't be trusted. You've been lying to me since day one."

"No, I haven't," Azure argued, unable to hold her tongue any longer. "I've been up front about everything. I haven't lied to you."

"You lied about your name, about why you wanted to interview me, and now you're lying about your anonymous source. Did your boss put you up to this, or did you plot my family's demise on your own?"

Azure reached for him, to caress his face, to give him a

physical reminder of the love they shared, but Harper stepped back, out of reach.

"Don't touch me."

"Baby, don't do this."

Harper angled his body away from her. His father's words came back to him. *Reporters are sneaky, cutthroat types who'll do anything for a headline. And your wife works for Leland Watson. That man would sell out his own mama for a story.*

The truth struck, smacked him upside the head like a rac-quetball.

Of course Azure was in cahoots with her source! She'd been trying to dig up dirt on his family from day one, but he'd been too busy lusting after her to take the threat seriously. But it wasn't too late. He could fix this. His family meant everything to him and he wasn't going to let Azure, or her evil, malicious boss, destroy his father's reputation.

"We can get past this, Harper. I know we can."

"Get past what?" he repeated, a disgusted expression on his face. "Our wedding was a publicity stunt to generate head-lines, remember? Quit acting like this is a real marriage. It's not."

Her legs gave way, buckled under the weight of his cruel taunts. Azure felt her eyes water and blinked hard to stop the tears from flowing. "Harper, you're the most important person in my life, and I want a future with you. Baby, I love you more than I've ever loved anyone, and I would never, ever do anything to jeopardize our relationship."

Harper pointed to the door. "Get out. Our business is through, and so are we."

"Baby, you don't mean that. You're just upset." Azure was burning up, and she couldn't slow her erratic heartbeat. The thought of leaving, of bailing on Harper when he needed her most had never crossed her mind. "Let's drop it for now. We can discuss this later, when we get back from Common's album release party—"

"I'm not going."

"Fine, we'll stay home." Azure gestured to the stack of take-out menus beside the phone. "What do you want for dinner? Chinese? Moroccan? Greek?"

"Pack your bags. I want you gone by the morning." Turning his back to her, he scooped his cell phone up off the table and strode off.

"Where do you expect me to go? Maggie and her boyfriend—"

"I don't care where you go. You're not welcome here anymore and I want you out."

The matter decided, Harper stalked out of the kitchen, leaving Azure all alone. She was beyond scared, and her trembling body proved it. The thought of being without Harper, the only man she'd ever truly loved, was terrifying.

To ward off an emotional breakdown, Azure squeezed her eyes shut and took a deep, cleansing breath. One didn't work, so she took two more. Her heart was broken, shattered into a million little pieces, but Azure willed herself to keep it together. There'd be plenty of time to cry later, to lament the loss of the man she loved, but right now she had to go upstairs and pack. Because after her explosive argument with Harper, she was not only hurting, but she was homeless.

Chapter 20

Azure awoke with a start. Disorientated, and half-asleep, she groped around the rickety side table for her ringing cell phone. Scooping it up with her hands, she tossed aside the stiff flower-printed blanket and swung her legs over the side of the queen-size bed.

Praying it was Harper, she cleared her throat and pressed the phone to her ear. The line was cutting in and out, and a shrill sound whirled in the background. To improve the connection, Azure stood and paced the length of her motel room. "Hello? Hello? Harper, are you there?"

"How are you doing, honey?"

Azure frowned. "Dad?"

"I better turn off the weed whacker. I can barely hear you!"

Waves of disappointment crashed down on her. Dropping onto the tacky plaid couch, her shoulders hunched in defeat, Azure took a moment to compose herself. The past seventy-two hours had been depressing, the most miserable time of her life. Harper wasn't taking her calls or responding to her text messages and emails. And if not for checking his Facebook page, she wouldn't know how he was doing. *Why hasn't he called? Doesn't he miss me? Not even a little?*

"Alice, are you still there?"

"Yeah," she said, mustering all the enthusiasm she had, "I'm still here."

"Is your husband around? I'd like to formally welcome him to the family."

"Sorry, Dad, um, Harper isn't here." Azure didn't want her parents—or anyone else—to know that Harper had kicked her out. Every day she went to work with a big, fat smile on her face and gushed about how wonderful married life was. But inside, she was dying a slow death. *How am I supposed to fix things if he won't talk to me?* Azure wondered, swallowing a sob.

"I'm looking forward to seeing you guys next month," Mr. Ellison said, his voice now loud and clear. "Alice, you think Harper can get me courtside tickets to the Sixers game?"

Panic seized her, drenched her skin with sweat. She couldn't let her parents come visit. Not now. Harper was mad at her, and she hadn't seen or heard from him in days. Azure would love to see her parents, but until she made up with Harper, she had to keep them in Tampa and out of Philly. "You guys can't come visit next month. I'm going out of town on assignment."

"For three weeks?"

"Yeah, I'm, uh, doing an in-depth interview with…with… Demetri Morretti."

"The slugger with the golden arm and lightning-quick speed?"

Azure felt like a fraud, and as she spun a tale sure to impress her dad, she wondered if the accusations Harper had made were true. Azure loved her husband, and her family, and didn't want to hurt them. That's why she told the occasional little white lie. But when her dad asked for an autographed baseball to add to his prized collection, her guilt was so strong, so powerful, Azure felt as if she'd been socked in the stomach. Maybe Harper was right. Maybe it was time she stop trying to be everything to everybody and speak her truth. No matter what.

"So, you're not upset about missing the charity gala for the Tuck Me In Foundation?" she asked.

"I was only going for your sake," Mr. Ellison confessed with a chuckle. "I'd rather play golf than schmooze with the rich and boogie any day!"

"Tell Mom I'm really sorry. I'll make it up to you guys soon."

"You can tell her yourself. She's right here. Sheryl, come get the phone. It's Alice!"

"No, Dad, it's okay—"

"Hi, honey! I was just thinking about you."

Azure sighed. Why couldn't her dad just pass on her message? "Hey, Mom. What are you up to? Puttering around in your garden again?"

"I sure am, and once your dad gets rid of all those pesky weeds, I'm going to have the best-looking rosebushes on the block," she explained, her voice dripping with pride. "But enough about my garden. Let's talk about you. What does your gown look like?"

"My gown?"

"Yes, the one you're wearing to the charity gala. I hope you didn't buy anything strapless or backless, because you don't have the right shape to pull off that style."

"Don't hold back, Mom. Tell me how you really feel," Azure mumbled, staring up at the hideous, canary-yellow ceiling.

"What kind of mother would I be if I didn't tell you the

truth?" she asked, her tone high-pitched. "I watched your interview on *City Spotlight* and was stunned to see how chubby you looked. You've only been married a couple weeks, but you're packing on the pounds!"

"Relax, Mom, I haven't gained any weight. It was just the cut of the dress."

"The camera doesn't lie, Alice!"

Azure rolled her eyes, and when her mom launched into her diet and nutrition spiel, she decided it was time to end the call. She never worked on weekends, but the thought of staying inside her small, dingy motel room all day was depressing. Azure wished Maggie wasn't out of town with her boyfriend, Greg. She needed someone to talk to, someone she could trust, and although she'd hit it off with Harper's cousin Marissa and Jake's fiancée, Charlotte, Azure didn't feel comfortable confiding in either one of them.

"You don't want to be one of those brides who gets married and then just lets themselves go," her mother warned. "Harper Hamilton is an attractive, successful attorney who probably has women throwing themselves at him all day long, and if you don't want him to leave you for someone younger and *thinner,* you better quit stuffing your face and head to the nearest gym."

"Mom, stop! Just stop it!" Azure yelled, knocking over the coffee table as she surged to her feet. Years of hurt, pain and frustration spilled out of her mouth, and when she was finished unburdening her heart, she felt emotionally drained. "I'm sick of you criticizing my appearance and putting me down. There's nothing wrong with me. Harper loves me just the way I am, and more importantly, I love myself."

"Alice, honey, relax. You're yelling—"

"And you're being mean," she tossed back, giving voice to her anger.

"I—I—I didn't mean to upset you. I was only trying to help."

"That's just it, Mom. You're *not* helping. I don't need you to be my dietician or my stylist, or my virtual trainer, either. All I need is for you to be my mom. That's it."

After a moment of silence, Mrs. Ellison said softly, "I can do that."

Azure felt her heart rate slow and an overwhelming sense of pride and relief flow through her. Being with Harper—a man who praised and encouraged her every day—had bolstered her confidence and given her the strength she needed to stand up to her mother. And from now on, she wasn't going to let anyone mistreat her.

"Maybe when I come visit next month we could spend the afternoon together doing girlie stuff. We could make it a mother-daughter day."

"No, thanks," Azure quipped, refusing to even entertain the idea. "The last time you suggested a mother-daughter day we ended up at that health and wellness ranch in Pensacola. I like to exercise, but those grueling, three-hour hikes almost killed me!"

Mrs. Ellison spoke with a smile. "I know you'll be busy helping out during the charity fundraiser, but I'd still like us to spend some quality time together while I'm in town."

Azure opened her mouth, but her conscience wouldn't let her repeat the lie she'd told her dad about going out of town on assignment next month. Admitting the truth was going to make her look like a failure in her mom's eyes, only confirming what her mother had always believed, but Azure didn't care. Thanks to Harper, she was confident in who she was and could defend herself. "You can't come to visit, Mom. Harper kicked me out and I'm staying in a cheap motel."

"What happened, honey? Talk to me, Alice. I want to help."

Comforted by her mother's words, she told her about the

explosive argument she'd had with Harper and the countless phone calls she'd made to his cell over the past three days. This was the kind of relationship Azure had always longed to have with her mom, one where she could share, and although being away from Harper made her heart ache, she was glad she could confide in her mom. "I don't know what to do anymore. He's completely shut me out."

"He needs some time to cool off," Mrs. Ellison explained, her tone softened with understanding. "You should come down here for a few days. Getting out of Philly will help clear your mind, and it would be great if you came to celebrate your dad's birthday with us."

"That might not be a bad idea," Azure thought out loud. "I could come for the weekend."

Mrs. Ellison whooped for joy. "Your dad would be thrilled. It will be the first time in years that you and your sister were both here for his birthday."

"Eden's there?"

"Yes, she got in last night. She's doing a photo shoot for *Shape* magazine this afternoon, and her agent got her a small role in an independent movie being filmed in Prague next month."

"That's great!" Azure cheered, wandering over to the window and gazing out at the bright morning sky. "I told Eden she had nothing to worry about."

"Your sister told me about her meltdown, Alice. I'm glad you were there for her. I know you girls haven't always gotten along, but now that you're older, I'm hoping you'll support and encourage each other more."

"Me, too, Mom."

Azure heard her father's voice in the background, and a muffled sound on the line.

"I wish we could talk some more, but I have to go get

cleaned up. I'm dragging your father to the symphony to-night, and I have a Vanessa Hamilton gown to squeeze into!"

Azure laughed for the first time all day. Standing up for herself, finally after all these years, was liberating, inspiring. And if she could tell her mom the truth, she could do any-thing—including work things out with Harper.

Shooting across the room, Azure grabbed her leather suit-case and heaved it onto the bed. She was going to take a shower, put on that black, belted suit that Harper loved so much—the one she was wearing the day she interviewed him at his family's Integrity estate—and head over to Ham-ilton, Hamilton and Clark. And this time, Azure was going to make Harper listen to her. No matter what.

Four hours later, Azure's body was chilled to the bone, and not just because she was sitting outside Harper's house in her small, two-door car. Cranking up the heat, she rubbed her ice-cold hands together. Azure wanted to go inside Harper's house and relax by the fire while she waited for him to return home from work, but he was still mad at her and she didn't want to make things worse between them.

I never imagined I'd one day be on a stakeout, Azure thought, cleaning the steamy windows with her hands and peering down the street for any signs of Harper's sleek black Lexus. With every passing second, Azure grew more anx-ious, more nervous.

Her mind slipped back to that afternoon, to the moment she stood outside the municipal courthouse waiting for Harper. After calling his office and learning from his secretary that he was in court, she'd headed right over. Dressed up, her hair styled just the way Harper liked, she'd been confident that he'd be willing to finally speak to her. And when Azure saw Harper stride out of the courthouse in a killer black suit, with Griffin Jackson at his side, her heart had skipped three beats. He'd looked right at her. Straight into her eyes. But instead of waving or acknowledging her presence with a smile, he'd continued right past her. As if she weren't there. Azure had been so shocked, so positively stunned, she didn't know what to do. And by the time she came to her senses, Harper had crossed the street and climbed into Griffin's silver truck.

On the drive back to the motel, she'd replayed the scene in her mind a dozen times. Maybe she was wrong. Maybe Harper didn't see her. It was possible, right? But deep down, she knew. Knew that he'd blown her off.

Azure saw the kitchen light come on in Harper's house, and she threw open her car door. Gripping her jacket collar, she flew up the steps and jabbed the doorbell. The breeze whipped her hair around her face, and colorful, autumn leaves danced in the air. The door creaked open, and seeing Harper, standing in the foyer, casually dressed in workout clothes, made Azure's heart murmur in her chest. "Harper, open up, it's me!"

"What do you want?"

Azure tried the screen door, but it was locked. "Can I come in?"

"No. I've had a long day, and I'm about to go to bed."

"I came by the courthouse today."

Harper stood as stiff as a Roman statue.

"Baby, it's been three days." Azure heard the desperation in her voice and paused to get her emotions under control. "We need to sit down and discuss this. Let's get everything out in the open, so we can move on."

"I don't want to talk to you."

"But I haven't done anything wrong! Why don't you believe me?"

Looking stone-faced, not moving a muscle, he spoke in an eerily calm voice. "What you've done is unforgivable, and every time I think about you plotting with your boss to ruin my father, I feel like punching a hole in the wall."

Azure's mouth felt frozen stiff. She wanted to argue, to demand Harper open the door so they could talk inside, but she couldn't get her lips to form the words. Any hope she had of them working things out evaporated when Harper closed the door. Then to her dismay and disbelief, he turned off the porch light.

Left alone, in the darkness, Azure faced the bitter truth. In that moment, she knew. Knew that Harper had never loved her. Just because they had amazing chemistry, shared heartfelt talks into the wee hours of the morning and made love passionately before drifting off to sleep every night didn't mean they were destined to be together. They weren't. And his cold, callous behavior proved just that. *What made me think that Harper ever loved me?* Azure thought sadly, blinking back tears. He was only doing what lawyers did best: act.

Later, she'd have no recollection of returning to her car or the thirty-minute drive back to the motel, but what Azure did remember was Harper's harsh words and tone, and how he'd slammed his front door in her face. That image replaced all her cherished memories of Harper—the first magical kiss they had shared as husband and wife, the morning they had made love on his living room couch, the last time he'd cradled her tenderly in his arms.

Lying flat on her stomach on the motel bed, writing in her journal, Azure decided it was time to take action. Drastic action. That was the only way she was ever going to get over Harper. *If that's even possible,* she thought sadly. How could she ever get used to living without Harper? The man who was her soul mate, her one true love?

Leaving Philly is the answer, she told herself, ignoring the doubts that rose in her mind. It wasn't as though her boss, or anyone else at *Eminence* magazine, would miss her. Azure had never liked working for Leland, anyway, and couldn't believe the lengths she'd gone to to impress him. She would never take the Hamilton family scandal public, and had no intention of giving her boss the inside scoop, either. These days, Azure could hardly stand to be around him, and if she heard Leland say "Enough with the fluff pieces! Bring me the dirt!" at another staff meeting, she was going to quit on the spot.

The thought of leaving Philadelphia, her hometown and a city she loved so much, caused sadness to fill the depths of her soul. But she had to go, had to put the past behind her. She'd start over in Florida, or somewhere close to her parents, and Harper would move on to someone else. Guys like him always did. He had no shortage of female admirers, and with his looks, success and pedigree, it would only be a matter of time before she saw pictures of him and beautiful debutantes splashed across the society pages.

Azure thought back over their brief, three-week marriage and marveled at how much he'd come to mean to her. Though it was fabulous, she wasn't going to miss Harper's house, driving around town in his cushy car or all the perks that came with being Mrs. Harper Hamilton. She was going to miss the little things. Eating breakfast together, snuggling on the couch watching *The Game* on Tuesday nights and the way Harper reached for her in the middle of the night.

Staring down at her wedding ring, she twisted the gigantic, diamond-speckled rock around her fourth finger. Azure knew she would have to give it back to Harper, sooner, rather than later, but she couldn't bring herself to take it off. She loved her ring, and everything it had once stood for.

Closing her eyes, she dropped her head on her pillow. It was wet with tears, but the more Azure tried to control her emotions, the harder she cried.

Chapter 21

Eminence magazine was housed in a five-story building, only blocks away from Rittenhouse Square, and when Harper stepped off the elevator and into the sun-splashed lobby, he stopped to make sure he was in the right place. The exterior of the building was plain but plush furniture, low-hanging Venetian lights and leafy plants gave the office a chic, metropolitan feel. The petite receptionist, with the big hair and plump lips, greeted him with a toothy smile.

"Good morning, Mr. Hamilton," she said, lowering the mouthpiece on her headset. "I'll let Azure know that you're here—"

"I'm not here to see…" Harper trailed off, paused to swallow the hard lump in his throat. He couldn't bring himself to say her name. Not after her bitter betrayal. For the past week, he'd moped around the house, analyzing everything Azure had said or done over the past month. He couldn't help it, couldn't stop himself. He had to figure out how he could have picked the wrong woman, not once, but twice. This time, though, the pain was ten times worse. Everywhere he went reminded him of Azure, and he couldn't close his eyes without seeing her face.

"I'm here to see Mr. Watson," he explained, reuniting with his voice. "Can you point me in the direction of his office?"

"It's straight down the hall to your left. He has the great big corner office with the picture of Pam Grier in the window!"

Smiling his thanks, Harper nodded and strode down the narrow corridor. He unzipped his jacket and loosened the knot in his black, lightweight scarf. The Burberry scarf Azure had bought him weeks earlier. The one that held the faint scent of her perfume.

Harper gave his head a shake. He had to stay focused. Had to prepare to confront the man plotting to ruin his father. No more thoughts of Azure. Not now, not ever.

"Harper!"

At the sound of Azure's voice, his heart stopped. She was walking down the other end of the hall, practically running toward him now, her loose, bouncy curls tumbling around her pretty face. His mind told him to do one thing, but his body did another. Instead of blowing past her and into Leland's corner office, Harper stopped right in front of Azure. Close enough to smell her perfume, to touch her, to steal a kiss from her moist, pink lips.

Scared his desires would overtake him, he raised his gaze from her mouth to her eyes. Big mistake. Her eyes were big and wide, filled with excitement, and she was smiling brighter than she had been at their wedding ceremony. If that was at all possible. She'd been a vision that day, the most beautiful sight his eyes had ever seen.

"Harper, you came! Baby, I'm so glad to see you!"

"I came to see Leland," he said, trying not to notice how gorgeous she looked in her kimono-style dress and leather boots. "You didn't think I was going to sit back and let you and your evil boss destroy my father, did you?"

The smile slid off her lips, and tears filled her eyes.

Harper started to touch her, to take her into his arms, then remembered she was the enemy and stuffed his hands into his jacket pocket. "Now, if you'll excuse me, I have important business to attend to. Bye, *Alice*. Have a nice life."

At the end of the hall, he entered Leland's office, marched straight over to his desk and demanded a moment of his time. "You and I need to have a word."

Coffee splashed over the side of Leland's oversize black mug and drenched the papers scattered around his desk. "You scared me half to death," he grumbled, cleaning the mess with a mound of tissue. "What's got you all wound up? Trouble in paradise already?"

"If you publish that slanderous, unauthorized story in your magazine, I will sue you and this company for everything it's worth. Understand?"

Leland wore a sad face, but a grin was tickling the corners of his thin, chapped lips. "It's too late, Harper. The November issue has already been put to bed."

Harper clenched his fists. He was going to blow, to erupt like the volcano that destroyed the village of Pam Pau. Only his fury was directed at one person, and one person only— Leland "The Snake" Watson. "This is not an idle threat, Leland. I will sue you, and win. Know that."

"There's nothing I can do. My hands are tied."

Harper gestured to Leland's desk phone. "Call the printers and order them to stop."

"I don't have that kind of authority. Your wedding photos are going to be in next month's issue, and there's nothing you or anyone else can do about it."

"My wedding photos?"

"Yeah, your wedding photos," he repeated, cocking a brow,

"so refrain from dumping Azure until *after* the November issue hits the stands."

Harper didn't know what to say. Couldn't speak even if he wanted to. His tongue lay limp in his mouth, and it felt as if his lips were glued together.

"You know, I had a lot of hope for you two," Leland announced, leaning back in his leather swivel chair and steepling his thin hands. "I thought you and Azure would be married for at *least* seventy-two days!"

Harper hung his head. The truth shamed and silenced him. He'd never felt so low, never felt like such a complete idiot. Azure hadn't betrayed his trust; she'd been telling the truth all along. And what had he done? Tossed her out on the street, blew by her outside the municipal court building and slammed his front door in her face.

Disappointed in himself, for allowing his past hurts to affect his relationship with Azure, he expelled a breath of frustration. How could he have let something like this happen? How could he have hurt Azure? The only women he'd ever loved. He owed her an apology, and more, and if she ever found it in her heart to forgive him, he'd make it up to her. Spare no expense. Prove to her every day for the rest of his life that he valued and cherished her.

Rubbing his hands over his face, he closed his eyes and prayed for divine intervention. Because it was going to take a miracle for Azure to forgive him. On the walk over to her office, Harper rehearsed what he was going to say. But the more he tried to plan his speech, the more he struggled. This wasn't one of his legal cases. He couldn't plot, couldn't map out what he was going to say or do. He had to speak from his heart, had to confess his deepest feelings, and if that didn't work, he'd beg like a felon before the parole board.

Prepared for the fight of his life, he knocked on Azure's door. She was sitting behind her desk, staring at her computer screen, and when Harper saw her tearstained cheeks, he knew she'd overheard his conversation with Leland. That's what he got for shouting and carrying on like the disgruntled ex-star of *Two and a Half Men*.

"Can I come in? I need to talk to you."

"I think you said enough out in the hall."

"Please, Azure, I only need a minute of your time."

Azure kept her eyes on her computer screen. She was hurt and confused, and looking at Harper would be her downfall. Was he here because he loved her? Or because he wanted to patch things up and continue their marriage charade? He was sending more mixed signals than a broken-down satellite dish, and Azure was sick of trying to figure him out, sick of chasing after him. It was better they go their separate ways. Starting over in a new city was going to be difficult, likely the hardest thing she'd ever done, but Azure knew the only hope she had of getting over Harper was by making a clean break.

"You're leaving?" Harper gestured to the red travel packet sitting on the middle of her desk. "Where are you going?"

"It's none of your business."

"Azure, you have every right to be mad at me, to hate me. I don't fault you for that," he confessed, his voice a notch above a whisper. "I'm deeply ashamed of the way I treated you. That's not me. I'm not that kind of guy. I don't treat people badly, not even Jake, and everyone knows I can't stand him!"

Arching her shoulders, Azure turned away from her computer screen and clasped her trembling hands. Dry-eyed and composed, she opened her mouth, fully prepared to ask Harper to get the hell out of her office, but when she saw the anguished expression on his face and heard the despair in his tone, she swallowed her retort.

"I was a jerk. I messed up. I admit it. I let my temper get the better of me, but I'm here now, ready to make up for the pain I've caused, ready to be the man you need me to be."

"Our deal is off, remember? Now you're free to sell the rights to our story to—"

"I don't want a deal. I want a real marriage, with you, if you'll still have me."

Azure gave him a blank stare, remained quiet. He looked contrite and sounded sincere, but she couldn't shake the feeling that Harper was playing her, only apologizing so he could parlay their breakup into an even bigger news story later down the road. "Harper, you don't know what you want. Three days ago, you called me *and* our marriage fake, and today you're professing your undying love. Which one is it?"

"I pushed you away because I was afraid to trust you, afraid to love. I was scared that we wouldn't last, but living without you this week has been torture. I feel like I'm losing my mind. I can't eat, I can't sleep and I think about you all day long."

"For a man who claims to be inconsolable, you seem all right to me."

"Looks are deceiving."

"You're right about that, because you had no problem blowing by me outside the municipal court building on Friday," she pointed out. "No problem at all."

Harper winced, as if he was in physical pain.

"Do you have any idea how embarrassed I was when you walked off with Griffin and left me standing there?" Azure's eyes thinned, and her voice climbed. "I never imagined you of all people would treat me that way. I—I thought you loved me."

"I do, Azure, with all my heart."

"Then why would you publicly humiliate me?"

"Baby, I am so sorry. I wasn't thinking," he confessed, moving closer to the desk. "Instead of listening to you, I let my anger and my pride get the best of me."

"But what happens the next time you get mad at me? Are

you going to toss me out on the street with nowhere to go? Or ignore me when I try to reach out to you?"

Harper held up his hand, as if he was taking an oath. "No, never, I swear."

"Why should I believe you? You've done it before, Harper. What's to say you won't do it again?" The wounds from being humiliated and shunned as a child ran deep, and Azure didn't know if she could ever forgive Harper for rejecting her—not once, not twice, but three heartbreaking times. "I'm not perfect, and there was a time when advancing my career was all I cared about, but I would never, *ever* do the things you accused me of."

"I know, Azure, and I'm sorry. You're my family, my wife, I should have believed you."

"Well, sorry isn't good enough," she snapped, anger and hurt gaining control of her mouth. "We're through, so please leave. I have a move to organize."

"Do I have to get down on my hands and knees and beg? Is that what it's going to take to convince you that I love you and that I can't live without you?"

Staring down at her hands, she slid the diamond ring off her fourth finger, placed it in her palm and offered it to him. "Here's your ring."

On the outside, Azure remained cool and unfazed, but when Harper came around her desk and kneeled down in front of her, she felt her heart melt. Hope surged through her veins, made her think that they could work things out.

For a long, quiet moment, they sat together in perfect silence.

"Cupcake, I need you. Without you I feel lost, incomplete, like a cold, hard, empty shell," Harper uttered, stroking his thumb over her cheeks. "Please don't leave me, baby. Don't run away. I will never, ever mistreat you, or let anything come between us again. I swear."

At his words, Azure was reminded of the bitter argument that had caused the rift between them in the first place. *Should I keep the secret? Or tell the truth and risk losing Harper again? What if he lashes out at me?* Choosing to listen to her heart, instead of succumbing to her fears, Azure took a deep breath, then repeated word for word what her anonymous source had said. And when she was finished, Harper looked as if he'd been hit by a truck. His face crumbled, and his stiff body was cold to the touch.

"No, no, no," he said, furiously shaking his head. "It isn't true. It can't be. My dad would never cheat on my mom. What proof does this woman have?"

"She didn't offer any. She said it was time the whole world know the truth and hung up."

Harper closed his eyes and dropped his head in his sweat-drenched hands. Could it be true? Could his dad have cheated with his own brother's wife? Could Marissa really be his sister, and not his cousin?

"I've heard rumblings about my father's infidelity for years, but I never dreamed he'd be with my…my…" Harper couldn't finish his sentence, couldn't bring himself to speak the vicious, ugly rumor out loud. "Cheating on your spouse is an unconscionable thing to do, but to father a child with another woman is despicable, and if…if…my dad had an affair with my aunt Jeanette and Marissa is his daughter, I'll quit the firm and sever all ties with him."

"Don't do anything drastic, Harper. Give yourself time to sort things out," Azure said, caressing the hard contours of his handsome face. "If the rumor turns out to be true, it's going to affect not only your life, but the lives of your family members, and that's nothing to take lightly. Don't make any hasty decisions, baby. It would be a mistake."

Harper nodded, as if he was considering what Azure said, but he'd already decided to take swift and precise action. Tomorrow, when he got to the office, he'd go see Marissa and together they'd decide what to do. Harper only hoped she was strong enough to handle the truth. He'd bumped into her that morning, as she was leaving the office for court, and was stunned to see her disheveled appearance. Dark circles lined her eyes, her hair was a tangled mess and her movements were slow, sluggish. Had the anonymous source phoned her, too? Was that why she looked stressed out? Something was going on with his cousin, and he was going to get to the bottom of it. "Thanks for telling me the truth. I know it couldn't have been easy."

Harper wore a sad smile, one that tugged at Azure's heartstrings.

"This kills, but I wouldn't have wanted to find out any other way."

Lacing her fingers through his, she gave his hand a light squeeze. "Harper, we'll get through this, together. I promise. I will be there for you every step of the way, no matter what."

Spotting her diamond ring glistening on her lap, Harper picked it up and slid it back on her fourth finger. He'd struck gold the day Azure walked into his uncle's Integrity Estate and back into his life. She had his best interests in heart, and as long as he had Azure by his side, he could survive anything—including the fallout of his father's infidelity.

"You're my heart and soul, Cupcake, and I'll never take you or our marriage for granted again," Harper promised, cupping her cheeks and pulling her gently toward him. "I love you, and I plan to spend the rest of my life proving it to you."

Their lips came together in a sweet, passion-filled reunion.

Wrapping his wife up in his arms, Harper held her close to his chest and lavished her mouth with his love. He had the woman of his dreams, a sister designed especially for him, and nothing—not even discovering his father's cruel betrayal—could ruin this moment.

"I don't want to ever lose you, Azure."

"Baby, you won't. You're the only man I love, the only man I want to be with."

"Are you sure?" he asked, brushing a stray curl away from her face. "You're not going to change your mind and leave me for a smooth-talking baseball star worth billions, are you?"

A cheeky grin warmed her mouth. "Of course not. Basketball's more my sport!"

Chuckling, Harper tightened his hold around her waist and nuzzled his stubby chin against her neck. "What am I going to do with you, woman?"

"Love me, support me and be there for me during good times and bad."

"I can do that. I *will* do that." Harper showered soft, light kisses across her cheeks and lips. "I love you, Azure, and I plan to make you the happiest woman in Philly!"

"I love you, too, Harper. Have from the moment I saw you walking down the halls of Willingham Prep. I knew one day we'd be together, and today, all my hopes and dreams finally came true."

Azure kissed her husband on the lips, with all the passion and desire flowing through her. The kiss set off shivers in her body and a strong, deep-seated hunger she had never known. Her heart was overcome, filled to the brim with love and unspeakable joy. They were going to make it, and finally, for the first time in her life, Azure had what she'd always wanted: Harper Hamilton, a man who loved her unconditionally, love handles and all!

* * * * *

When it comes to matchmaking, will two longtime friends put their relationship on the line for the sake of love?

ESSENCE BESTSELLING AUTHOR

ADRIANNE BYRD

For ten years, lawyer Destiny Brockman saw her carefree—but very, very fine—neighbor Miles Stafford as just a good friend. So when she declares that there are no good men in Atlanta, Miles proposes a friendly wager: to set each other up on a date with the perfect match. But could the undeniable attraction that's been simmering between them for years bring the sweetest reward!

Available October 2012 wherever books are sold!

HARLEQUIN®
www.Harlequin.com

KPAB4891012

REQUEST YOUR FREE BOOKS!

2 FREE NOVELS
PLUS 2 FREE GIFTS!

KIMANI™
ROMANCE

Love's ultimate destination!

KROM11B

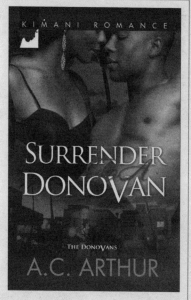

**A brand-new miniseries
featuring fan-favorite authors!**

THE HAMILTONS ⚖ *Laws of Love*

Family. Justice. Passion.

Ann Christopher	Pamela Yaye	Jacquelin Thomas
KIMANI ROMANCE	KIMANI ROMANCE	KIMANI ROMANCE
Case for Seduction	*Evidence of Desire*	*Legal Attraction*
Ann Christopher	Pamela Yaye	Jacquelin Thomas
Available September 2012	*Available October 2012*	*Available November 2012*

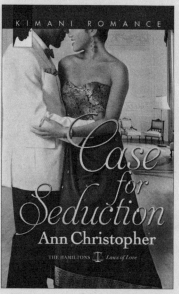 

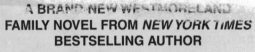

A BRAND-NEW WESTMORELAND
**FAMILY NOVEL FROM *NEW YORK TIMES*
BESTSELLING AUTHOR**

BRENDA JACKSON

Megan Westmoreland needs answers about her
family's past. And Rico Claiborne is the man to
find them. But when the truth comes out, Rico
offers her a shoulder to lean on…and much,
much more. Megan has heard that passions burn
hotter in Texas. Now she's ready to find out….

TEXAS WILD

"Jackson's characters are…hot enough to burn the pages."
—*RT Book Reviews* on *Westmoreland's Way*

Available October 2 from Harlequin Desire®.